THE TETHERING

THE TETHERING, BOOK ONE

MEGAN O'RUSSELL

Ink Worlds Press

Visit our website at www.MeganORussell.com

This book is a work of fiction. Names, characters, places, and incidents either are products of the author's imagination or are used fictitiously. Any resemblance to actual persons, living or dead, events, or locales is entirely coincidental.

The Tethering

Copyright © 2013, Megan O'Russell

Cover Art by Sleepy Fox Studio (https://www.sleepyfoxstudio.net/)

Editing by Christopher Russell

Interior Design by Christopher Russell

All rights reserved.

No part of this publication may be used or reproduced in any manner whatsoever without written permission, except in the case of brief quotations embodied in critical articles and reviews. Requests for permission should be addressed to Ink Worlds Press.

Printed in the United States of America

DEDICATION

To Chris, my coniunx

PROLOGUE

Seven Years Ago

*J*acob Evans sat in the front row, looking back whenever he could at the new girl two rows behind him. He didn't want her to catch him staring, but he couldn't help himself. A few times her eyes met his, but Jacob didn't care. None of the other kids in school had ever liked him anyway. What did it matter if the new girl thought he was rude?

He glanced at her again. She stared back at him and smiled. A beautiful smile that made him like the new girl.

Jacob never sat in the cafeteria to eat lunch. He would hide in the bathroom or find an empty classroom to eat in when the weather was bad. But today was beautiful, one of the first nice days of spring, so he found a big shady tree far away from the other students.

He had half a peanut butter sandwich for lunch today. Money was running low, and he couldn't even guess when his father would be back. Jacob huddled around his sandwich possessively, like a squirrel protecting a nut. People always stared at his meager lunch. Not to steal, but to judge, which felt much worse.

The new girl walked out of the cafeteria and onto the lawn with her shoulders hunched. Jacob couldn't tell if she was upset or just weighed down by the enormous lunch bag she carried. She looked at him and strode straight over, blowing her long black hair out of her eyes.

"Can I sit?" she asked.

Jacob nodded.

She let her giant lunch bag fall to the ground. "I'm Emilia." She held out her hand for Jacob to shake. "I'm in your class."

Jacob didn't move. He stared into Emilia's grey eyes. Why was she speaking to him? What did she want?

Emilia smiled before sitting and unpacking her lunch bag. She pulled out two sandwiches, carrots, apples, cookies, juice, milk, and what looked like an entire tray of brownies.

Jacob swallowed hard, willing his stomach not to growl. That was more food than he usually got to eat in a week.

"I told Molly not to pack me so much," Emilia said. "I think she was worried nobody would like me. Or maybe that I would starve to death my first day of school."

"Who's Molly?" Jacob asked. "Is she your sister?"

"No, she's the housekeeper and cook. And she takes care of me sometimes, when there's no one else around."

Jacob nodded, wishing he had a Molly to feed him when there was no one else around.

"She packed more than I could ever eat." Emilia held out a sandwich to Jacob. "She'll be heartbroken if I bring anything home."

Jacob looked at Emilia and knew she wasn't there to be mean or make fun. "I'm Jacob," he said quietly. And for the first time he could remember, he ate until his stomach was full, and he sat with a friend.

∾

Six Years Ago

*E*milia knew Jacob hated lightning storms, though she had never asked him why. Maybe it was because no one had ever comforted him during storms when he was very small. She could picture exactly where she would find him once she managed to climb onto the roof of the porch. Sitting at the head of his bed by his pillow, crushed up in the corner of the walls.

The porch lattice was slippery in the rain, so she took her time climbing up to his window. She tapped lightly before slipping her fingers into the crack and sliding the window open. She didn't bother to look around the room as she took off her raincoat and shoes, leaving them to drip on the stone-cold radiator without any hope they might actually dry. Finally, she peered through the darkness at the bed in the corner.

There sat Jacob, smiling through his fear because she had come for him.

She crept across the worn carpet, the boards beneath creaking with each step, then picked up his pillow, held it to her chest, and sat beside him. The next time lightning struck, he didn't flinch.

∾

Five Years Ago

*T*he cafeteria at Fairfield Middle School was particularly noisy that day. Jacob liked the noise. People were less likely to notice him.

He headed straight to a table in the far corner. No one ever went over there. No one but Emilia. Eating with her was the best part of his day. He sat and waited for her to come to him.

"Hi," Emilia said as she emerged from the crowd. She sat across from him and started organizing her lunch tray. She looked at Jacob and the empty table in front of him where his lunch should have been. "Your dad's still not back." It wasn't a question.

Jacob traced the graffiti on the table with his finger. He didn't like to talk about his father with Emilia. It ruined his time with her. He didn't like to think about bad things when she was around.

"Did you run out of money?" Emilia asked.

Jacob didn't answer. Whenever Jim left town for a job, he left behind some money. Jacob had learned over the years to be careful with it, to stretch it as far as he could. But occasionally he ran out anyway.

"Here." She cut her burger in half, passing him the larger of the two pieces.

"I'm fine." Jacob shook his head.

Emilia's right eyebrow arched as she stared him down. "There's no point in going hungry." She gave him her milk, too. "Come over after school, and we'll make up some grocery bags for you. Molly is making pizza tonight. You can stay for dinner."

Jacob looked away. Tears burned in his eyes. He hated pity.

Emilia reached over and grabbed his hand. "Jacob, don't. I was lucky when I got Aunt Iz. It's only right I share her with you."

~

Four Years Ago

*J*t was hot. That horrible kind of hot that seemed to make even Jacob's bones sweat. He lay on the floor of the living room underneath the ceiling fan. He watched as it swirled around. It didn't make the room cooler, but it kept the air moving, making it easier to breathe.

School would be starting again soon. Usually, Jacob dreaded

the start of school, but it had been so hot all summer, he had been daydreaming about sitting in an air-conditioned classroom.

This hadn't been his best summer on any account. Jim had left five days after school let out, and he hadn't been back since. Luckily, Jacob had gotten old enough he could find odd jobs around the neighborhood. He weeded for twenty dollars, mowed for fifteen. It wasn't much, but he had managed to keep himself fed.

The only good part of the summer was Emilia. Most days she would come over to get him, and they would go somewhere. Anywhere. To her house, to the park. He didn't care where they went as long as she was there.

Jacob closed his eyes and waited for the knock on the door. He loved that knock. It meant good things were about to happen.

He only had to wait a minute before the porch step squeaked. *Knock, knock, knock.*

⁓

*T*he water was wonderful and cool. Emilia ran through the trees, grabbed the long rope, and swung out over the deepest part of the water before letting go. The air shot from her lungs as she pushed herself up to the surface, laughing.

"Come on, Jacob!" she called.

But Jacob sat in the shallow water, shaking his head. "Emi, I don't think we should use the rope."

Emilia scrambled out of the water and ran back through the trees, the pine needles pricking her feet as she prepared to charge back to the rope.

"I don't think it's safe," Jacob shouted.

Emilia had already started running toward the water. She glanced back at Jacob, sticking out her tongue as she grabbed the rope. She soared out over the glistening water and knew something was wrong. The rope swung in an arc back over the rocky bank.

Emilia screamed as the rope slipped from her grasp. She felt her wrist snap, and something sharp pierced the top of her forehead when she hit the ground.

"Emi!"

There was splashing behind her.

"Emilia." Jacob knelt next to her.

She tried to sit up. The trees swam in front of her eyes, but everything looked red. Somehow strangely red.

"It's okay." Jacob wiped something from her face. A smear of red streaked his palm, and she knew it was blood. Her blood. "Everything is going to be okay."

Emilia forced her eyes to focus on Jacob. He was pale, and his eyes were wide.

"You're going to be fine," Jacob whispered.

Suddenly, a warmth moved up her fingers into her arm. Heat burned in the top of her head. She gasped at the pain shooting down through her skull.

And then it was gone. All the pain had vanished.

Tears glistened in Jacob's eyes and something else she had never seen before. Her lungs turned to lead.

"I'm fine, Jacob," Emilia said, trying not to choke on the fear that was drowning her. "I'm fine."

"*I* have to go."

"Please, Emilia, you can't do this." Jacob grabbed her hand, pulling her away from the window. "You can't leave me."

"I have to." Tears streamed down her face. "I'm sorry I can't explain, but I have to go."

"Then take me with you."

"I can't."

"Emi, please," Jacob begged, but Emilia pulled her hand away.

"No." Her voice broke. She needed to go now, while she could still make herself do it. She slipped her necklace over her head and pressed it into his hand. "I'll come back for you, I promise." She climbed out the window and onto the porch roof. "I'll come back for you as soon as I can. Don't forget me."

1
WINDOWS

*J*acob rolled over, unwilling to let the sound of his alarm tear him from his dream. He tried to hold on to the image of her, but it was already drifting away into memory. He reached out and turned off the alarm.

He hadn't dreamt about her in months. Not that he hadn't thought about Emilia. He did that every day. The memory of the day he had first met Emilia Gray, seven years ago now, was one of the best he had.

He rolled out of bed and stumbled to his dresser. He had changed a lot from the little boy hiding under a tree. Now sixteen, Jacob was one of the tallest boys in his class, though he still had the thin look of someone who had grown quickly in a short time. His hair was as blond and shaggy as ever, and he had developed a golden tan from working outside all spring.

"She's gone," he told himself. "Get used to it."

He dressed quickly, throwing on whatever smelled clean, and stopped on his way out the door to check in his father's room. Jim had been gone for a few months now, and since the bed was still made, Jacob assumed he hadn't come home last night.

"Great," he muttered, slamming the front door behind him on his way to another day at Fairfield High.

Fairfield, New York was a nice place. At least in Jacob's opinion. Of course, he had never actually been anywhere else. The town was small and picturesque, and the streets were always clean. With summer's approach, the only scent in town came from the iris blossoms that coated the town square. Planted in color-coordinated beds, they surrounded the gazebo that was regularly used to host town events. Signs rising above the blooms proudly stated the irises were a gift of the Ladies' Library League, the group of women who kept the town pristine and perfect.

The schools were excellent, the stores locally owned, and the houses well painted. Except for Jacob's house, which hadn't been painted in his lifetime. He tried to keep up the house as much as he could, but Jim didn't care enough to help. The Ladies' Library League always noticed, but what was Jacob supposed to do?

Jim had drifted from job to job ever since Jacob was two. That was the year his mother died. When Jacob was eight, Jim had started taking work away from Fairfield. He was hardly ever in town anymore. It was normal for him to disappear for months at a time, working...somewhere. He usually left some cash behind, but Jacob didn't care about Jim's money so much anymore. He'd been doing odd jobs for years, and now that he was older, people around town were willing to give him larger jobs with better paychecks. Thanks to a profitable spring, he'd had enough money not only to eat since the last time Jim had skipped town, but to keep the electricity and water on, too. Jacob laughed to himself. That had been a feat.

No one greeted him when he walked into Fairfield High, but he didn't mind. Anonymity suited him. School was a means to an end, and Jacob wanted out. Out of Jim's house, out of Fairfield. But most of all, he wanted to be good enough for her.

Jacob had made up his mind freshman year that he was going to be the best in the whole school. He was going to get a scholarship, go to college, and make something worthwhile of himself. Days at school flew by. Teachers loved him. Students ignored him. It was perfect.

Jacob sat in chemistry class, allowing his mind to wander. He had already read through the entire book, and the lectures were useless since his teacher insisted on reading from the book verbatim every day.

There was a cough at the door.

Jacob looked over with the rest of his classmates, hoping something would break the monotony.

Principal McManis stood in the doorway, his hands flitting between his watch and glasses. He seemed like a decent guy, and Jacob liked him, so he gave an encouraging smile.

The principal did not smile back. "Jacob Evans, I need to see you in my office."

Sweat beaded on Jacob's palms. He could feel the eyes of his classmates burning holes into his face. He got up to follow the principal.

"Bring your bag."

That wasn't a good sign. Bring your bag meant he was in so much trouble he wouldn't be returning to class, or maybe even to school, for quite a while. But Jacob was always very careful to stay out of trouble. If the school wanted to talk to his father about his behavior, they would find out how often Jim was gone. Then Social Services would be all over him.

Jacob picked up his bag and carefully repacked his chemistry book before starting toward the door. Every time he passed a desk, its occupant started to whisper. By the time he reached the principal, the room sounded like a balloon slowly letting out its air.

Jacob's worn sneakers squeaked as he walked down the hall, and McManis's loafers clacked like they were made of the same worn tile as the floor. The sound of their shoes echoed through the corridor like a siren, telling every room they passed that someone was being led to the principal's office. Not once did McManis look over at Jacob.

McManis ushered Jacob into his office and shut the door. Windows surrounded the room, looking out at the secretary's office and the locker-lined hallways. The secretary kept glancing through the window at Jacob. When he caught her eye, she quickly began shuffling papers on her desk.

"Please sit down." Principal McManis took a seat behind his desk, still avoiding Jacob's eyes. He took a drink from his *#1 Educator* mug, set it down, and rubbed his thumb along the rim, wiping away something Jacob couldn't see.

Was McManis waiting for him to speak or just buying himself time?

"Look," Jacob said, "whatever you think I did, it must have been someone else. You know I would never—"

"This isn't..." McManis paused. "I'm—there was an accident."

Jacob stared at his principal. If there was an accident, why was he in trouble?

"I'm afraid I have some bad news," the principal said, studying his hands. "Your father was found in a hotel room. They aren't sure yet how it happened." He finally met Jacob's eyes. "I'm afraid he's gone."

Jacob's heart stopped. His brain started to scream. All of the bones in his body burned. McManis was still talking, but Jacob couldn't make out the words over the screaming in his head.

A sharp *snap* slammed into his ears right before the windows in the office exploded, sending shards of glass everywhere. The shrieking in his mind was punctured by more glass breaking, more windows flying apart. He stared down at the bits of glass shimmering on the floor.

He gasped as the principal knocked him to the ground, covering Jacob with his own body. Other screams echoed in the distance. It took Jacob a moment to figure out the panicked screaming wasn't in his head. As the fire alarms started wailing,

Jacob tried to push himself up to see what was happening, but Principal McManis forced him back down.

Voices cut through the mayhem as teachers tried to calm their students. Students shouted for help, not knowing what to do.

The principal cursed. "Stay here, Jacob. Do not leave this room until a fireman or I tell you to. Got it?" McManis didn't wait for an answer as he shoved Jacob under the desk.

The shattered pieces of the *#1 Educator* mug cut into Jacob's palms, and the smell of spilled coffee filled the air. The coffee puddle was warm, and he watched with fascination as his red blood mixed with the brown liquid.

Jacob listened to Principal McManis order a school lockdown. The *thud* of doors slamming shut echoed down the hall. A few moments later, McManis's voice came back over the speakers, saying to evacuate as quickly as possible. A school with broken windows couldn't be locked down.

Jacob waited in the office for McManis. A few minutes passed before the principal returned for Jacob and led him outside to the rest of his class. Jacob was almost grateful for the confusion when the fire trucks arrived. No one stopped him or asked if he was all right. He blended perfectly into the chaos.

The emergency workers set up triage sites for the injured, but no one had been badly hurt. A few students needed stitches, and some were so panicked they had to be sedated, but there were no real injuries.

The police bomb squad swept through the building but found nothing. They checked for a gas leak, but the lines all seemed to be in good working order. The rumblings in the crowd said the police were at a loss to explain how every piece of glass in the building had shattered. No one was allowed to leave.

At what should have been dinnertime, all of the students' parents who had rushed to the school brought them food. But Jacob had no one who cared that his school had apparently been *attacked by terrorists*. At least that's what the news reporter nearest him told her viewers at home. A woman from a church group gave Jacob water, food, and a blanket at about nine o'clock in the evening, and he was too tired to refuse.

Finally, the police said they'd gathered all the information they needed, which was none at all, and that they would be in touch with updates.

Jacob started to walk home. Principal McManis's booming voice carried over the crowd, calling Jacob back, but he kept walking. Social Services would come for him soon enough.

The lights were off in the house, but Jacob was used to that. He was used to being alone. He opened the creaky door and sat down on the couch. This may not have been a happy home, but it was the only one he knew. He looked around the living room. The dingy wallpaper peeled away at the corners. A faint scent of dust and damp hung in the air. Jacob kept the house clean, but Jim never gave him the money to fix anything. The couch he sat on was older than he was. The stained fabric glistened in places where the springs were beginning to wear through.

He should be doing something. Like planning a funeral. But he didn't even know where Jim's body was. Not that he had the money to pay for a funeral anyway. Sleep. He needed sleep. Everything else could be handled tomorrow.

Jacob climbed the stairs to his room. Out of habit, he looked into Jim's room. It was the same as it had been that morning with the bed still untouched. For some reason, Jacob had expected it to look different, as though permanent absence would leave a visible mark. He pulled Jim's door closed and went to his own bed.

He didn't even remember closing his eyes, but a steady tapping that echoed through the empty house pulled him back out of sleep. He dragged the blanket the woman from the church group had given him over his head. He wanted sleep, not social workers.

But the tapping continued. It sounded closer than the front door. Maybe it was hail. No, the sound was too regular for hail.

Jacob sat up and looked blearily around his room. The sound came from the window. A figure crouched outside, tapping lightly to wake him up.

2

THE MANSION HOUSE

*J*acob tossed off the blanket, ran to the window, and threw it open.

And there she was. Emilia Gray.

She pushed herself through the window and threw her arms around Jacob's neck. "Jacob," she said, her voice full of pain and concern. "I'm so sorry."

Jacob froze for a moment, unsure if he was actually awake, until the cool night air whispered through Emilia's hair, carrying with it the soft scent of lilacs. "Emi?" he whispered, wrapping his arms around her. She felt warm and incredibly real.

She pulled away to look him in the eye. "I came as soon as I heard everything that happened. Are you all right?"

"I'm—" Jacob reached up and touched Emilia's face, brushing a strand of long black hair from her forehead. "You're here?" His voice sounded raw. "Are you really here?"

"I'm really here," Emilia said. "I came back for you. I promised I would. Jacob, I'm sorry."

He pulled her into his arms and buried his face in her hair, trying hard to remember how to breathe. She hadn't changed that much. Her hair was long and black, and her eyes were misty grey. She was taller now but still her. Still perfect.

"Are you okay?" Emilia whispered.

"I'm fine." Jacob pulled away and ran a hand through his hair, trying to stop his head from spinning. "I think I might be in shock or something. I'm so used to Jim being gone. I guess I just don't understand that he isn't coming back. Is that weird?"

"I don't think so."

"How did you know?" Jacob asked. "How did you know about Jim so fast? I mean, I only found out this morning."

"I know, and I know this is an awful time. But I had to come now before it was too late."

"He's dead. I don't think there's really a time crunch," Jacob said with a hoarse laugh. The laugh caught in his throat and turned unexpectedly into a sob. He tried to breathe, but it only made the sobs louder.

Emilia pulled him over to the bed and curled up in the corner, putting Jacob's head on her shoulder.

Jacob didn't know how long he had cried, but he hurt everywhere. He hurt like he had run a marathon. His throat was dry, and his eyes stung. He stayed sitting next to Emilia on the bed. She had held him as he cried for losing the father who was never there. As Emilia reached up to wipe a tear from his cheek, he vowed he would never cry for Jim again. It was over. Jim was gone.

Jacob took a deep breath. "Thank you." He looked down at Emilia's hand holding his.

"I'm so sorry, but we can't stay here." She silenced Jacob's protest. "I didn't come here because of your father. I came to get you. Just like I promised I would. It's time now," she said slowly. "I am so sorry about Jim, but I need you to come with me."

Something wasn't right. Emilia was here in his room. They were together, but she looked worried. Almost frightened.

"I came because of what happened at your school. What you did to your school."

Jacob shook his head as her words sank in. "Is that what the police are saying? I was with Principal McManis when it happened. It wasn't me." Panic crept into his chest. He looked around his bedroom, sure the police were going to break in at any moment to arrest him.

"The police think it was some sort of terrorist attack. I love how they can invent logical explanations for just about anything." Emilia pulled Jacob back when he started toward the window to look for police cars. "They don't suspect you at all."

Jacob searched Emilia's eyes, unsure if he should be relieved or more afraid. Who else but the police would come for him?

"But we know you did it," Emilia said. "You broke all those windows. Well, every piece of glass in the building actually."

"What do you mean I broke the windows?"

"Jacob. You are special. Different, like me. You have abilities you don't understand, but when you're upset—"

"What are you talking about?"

"Magic, Jacob. Wizardry, sorcery, *maleficium*, whatever you want to call it. I'm a witch, you're a wizard, and we need to get out of here."

Jacob stared at Emilia. He ran his hand over her cheek.

She grabbed his hand. "Jacob, I'm real. And this is real. There is a whole world out there. A magical world. But you have to decide right now if you want to be a part of it. There are things in my world that are beyond your imagination, but if you come with me, you can never go back to being normal. You can never come back here."

"Emi." Jacob shook his head. "This is crazy."

She brought his hand between them. It was covered in small cuts from shards of McManis's mug. His hand warmed in her grasp. Not unpleasantly so, but as though it were submerged in warm water. Then his skin tingled and stung. The places where the skin had been broken became almost iridescent. Finally, the glow subsided, and the cuts started to fade. After a few seconds, his hand had completely healed.

"It is real." Emilia stared into Jacob's eyes. "Will you come with me?"

Jacob couldn't think beyond Emilia's return. He was tired, and his brain felt fuzzy. His school was wrecked. His father was dead.

He wanted to be angry with Emilia. To shake her for making him even more confused, to yell at her for disappearing for four years, and for clearly having left out some very important details in the course of their friendship. He didn't understand what was happening.

Emilia's hands were so delicate in his. He would do anything to keep her from disappearing again. He would follow Emilia Gray to the ends of the earth.

"Do I need to pack anything?" he asked.

"Only if you want to." Emilia gave him a hard, serious look. "Jacob, are you sure this is what you want?"

"Yes."

Emilia offered to help him pack, but there wasn't very much Jacob wanted to take with him. He already had everything important packed in a box under his bed. Pictures of his parents. A book his mother had written her name in. All of the notes his father had left on the kitchen table every time he went out of town. Jacob kept the box packed in case a social worker came for him. All he had to do was throw some clothes into a bag, and he was ready to go.

He turned off the lights and walked out the front door. He hesitated with the key in his hand for a moment before leaving it in the lock. Under the streetlight, a very shiny black car waited for them.

Jacob didn't look back as he walked to the car. He didn't need to. There was nothing left for him there.

Emilia opened the car door for him.

"Nice to see you, Jacob," Samuel, the Grays' driver and gardener, spoke from the front seat. "I am very sorry for your loss."

Jacob nodded, studying Samuel's reflection in the rearview mirror. Samuel had dust-brown hair and laugh lines that never faded. But there were new, harsh lines around his eyes and forehead Jacob had never seen before. Lines that hadn't come from Samuel's constant knowing smile.

Emilia climbed into the car. "If we hurry, we might make it before everyone wakes up."

"Somehow I think there'll still be trouble," Samuel said as they drove away from Fairfield.

"Where are we going?" Jacob asked when Samuel turned the car onto the highway. Since Emilia had left, he had only been on the highway twice for school trips. It was strange to see the night whisking by at sixty-five miles per hour.

"To the Mansion House. It's about two hours away." Emilia chewed her bottom lip. Jacob recognized that worried look. "Aunt Iz might be awake when we get back. She didn't want me to come with Samuel, but I convinced him I had to come. I wanted to get you myself."

"Two hours away." Jacob shook his head. "Two hours away and you never once came to see me?" His head started to spin again. As the minutes ticked past, things made less and less sense.

Emilia looked at him with pain in her eyes. "It wasn't my choice. It's so complicated, and it's not supposed to be me who explains. There are rules that can never be broken. At the house, you believed me when I told you you're a wizard. Now you have to believe me when I tell you there are rules and responsibilities that come with those powers."

"Powers." Jacob rubbed the skin on his palm that had been healed less than an hour ago. "Powers?"

Emilia shook her head. "Not now. You should sleep."

He didn't want to close his eyes and risk her being gone again when he opened them. The first rays of light crept over the mountains. He had a hundred questions. Where had she been? What was he capable of? But really, he was too tired to push for answers. So he sat with his fingers laced through hers and watched the sunrise.

They crossed the border into Massachusetts and drove through a small town. A paperboy pedaled past on his morning route, the sole inhabitant moving down the sleepy streets on his bicycle. Would Jacob's school or his father's death be in the newspaper?

They drove past the town and onto a smaller road lined so thickly with trees it was impossible to see more than a few feet on either side of the car. Samuel turned the car left onto a driveway no one would notice if they didn't know exactly where to look. A hundred feet down the drive, they came to a tall stone wall surrounding the property. A set of iron gates etched with strange symbols swung open. The car shuddered as it passed through the gates.

Emilia squeezed his hand. "Don't worry. It's just the *fortaceria*. A spell to turn outsiders away."

Jacob nodded, amazed he hadn't been rejected by the gate.

The driveway was so long and the trees so large, at first he couldn't see the house at all. When the building finally came into view, Jacob had to agree with its name. It was a mansion. Not anything hugely luxurious, but delicate and stately. Definitely larger than any of the houses in Fairfield, but somehow it still seemed homey.

As they stopped in front of the house, several people came running through the front door at once. They called to the car, but Jacob couldn't make out their words over the *crunch* of the gravel. First out of the door was a dark-haired boy, tall and muscled, who seemed to be the same age as Jacob. Then a small, blond girl of maybe eleven or twelve, still wearing her pink pajamas. A red-haired boy came next, dragging Molly, the Grays' cook. Last came an older man, small and toady, wearing a maroon bathrobe. He had Aunt Iz on his arm. She was, of course, smiling her wry smile as the car stopped.

The dark-haired boy ran to open Emilia's door. Jacob thought he heard Emilia whimper as the boy reached in and pulled her from the car.

The boy crushed her to his chest. "What the hell were you thinking? Do you have any idea—"

"Dex, I'm sorry," Emilia said, "but I had to go—"

"Go running into the epicenter of an incident like this? Do you know what could have happened to you?"

"Yes, Dexter, I do. That's why I had to go." Emilia pulled herself away. She glanced at Jacob in the car. "Please, Dex," she whispered in a voice almost too quiet for Jacob to hear.

Dexter brushed Emilia's hair off her face and kissed her before pulling her back into his arms.

3

ON THE BRINK

*A*ll of the air had been sucked out of the world. There was no air in Jacob's lungs and no air left for him to inhale.

Emilia broke away from Dexter and took Jacob's hand. She smiled at him as though nothing were strange or wrong. She drew Jacob out of the car and led him to the steps, where the rest of the welcoming committee waited.

"Everyone, this is Jacob. Jacob, this is Claire Wren." She indicated the little blond girl. "And Connor Wright, Molly's nephew." The red-headed boy waved. "Professor Eames." The man next to Aunt Iz bowed. "And Dexter Wayland," she said, looking back at the boy who had just kissed her.

Dexter walked up to Jacob and shook his hand. "It's a pleasure to finally meet you." As they let go, Dexter wrapped his arm around Emilia's waist, inserting himself firmly between her and Jacob.

Jacob thought he saw a gleam in Dexter's eye before Molly pulled him into a back-breaking hug.

"It's so good to see you again, Jacob. Let me see." Molly held Jacob at arm's length and tutted noisily. "Well, you need to be fed up a bit, and your hair needs cutting."

Then Aunt Iz was upon him. She held his face in her hands and looked straight into his eyes, as though she were seeing everything that had happened in the last few years just by staring at him with that deep, penetrating gaze.

Iz smiled sadly and nodded before turning back to the rest of the group. "A strong cup of tea and some food in my study, Molly. Connor, please take his things to the green room. And yes, Claire, you may see to the closet."

Claire squealed with delight and grabbed Jacob's backpack from Connor before darting into the house.

"Samuel," Iz called to the driver, "get some sleep before you go, and try to keep her under control."

Samuel nodded.

As the car pulled away, Iz turned back to Jacob. "Come to my study. There are quite a few things we need to discuss." Iz held up a finger, stopping Emilia when she tried to follow them into the house. "No, Emilia, I will speak to Jacob alone. You and I shall have a little chat later."

Iz didn't yell, but her tone left no doubt Emilia was in serious trouble.

Jacob glanced back as he followed Iz into the house, his stomach disappearing as Dexter kissed Emilia again.

The inside of the Mansion House was as lovely as the outside. Early morning light poured in from every direction. A grand cherry staircase cut through the center of the house. The air smelled like wood and cooking. Very good home cooking.

Iz led him down the hall to a large cherry door. A barren tree with branches that reached to the sky and roots that dug deep into the ground had been carved into the wood.

Jacob touched the symbol.

"It's the crest of the Gray Clan," Iz said as she opened the door to her study. She gestured for Jacob to sit.

"I've seen it before," he said. "On the ring Emilia always wore."

"Very good." Iz smiled. "I gave that ring to Emilia on her seventh birthday, and she still wears it all the time."

Molly came in with food. While she sorted the tray, Jacob looked around Iz's study. He sat on a plush green chair. Iz's desk and the table with the food were both carved of the same rich cherry wood that adorned the rest of the house. Books of all sizes lined the walls, and a large mirror had been set into a recess in the corner next to a shining black piano.

Finally, Molly left, and Iz handed him a cup of tea and a fresh biscuit. "Molly is right. You could do with some feeding up." Iz sat behind her desk.

The room was as different as could be, but Jacob still felt like he was back in Principal McManis's office.

"Eat." Iz sipped her own tea.

Jacob just nodded. He didn't know what to say. "Thank you for breakfast," was all he could manage a few mouthfuls later.

"I am sorry for all you have been through," Iz said. "And I deeply regret my family was not there to help you through the last few years. We all care for you very much. Leaving you behind in Fairfield was not an easy decision. Although, I am sure you can now see that we did have a very good reason for our abrupt departure."

"'Cause I'm a wizard?" Jacob asked.

"Because you are indeed a wizard."

"What does that even mean?"

"It means you have the ability to do things far outside the realm of possibility for humans," Iz said.

"You have the ability to affect the world around you with your mind and your energy," said a voice from behind him.

Iz's voice. It was Iz's voice Jacob had heard behind him, but she was still sitting at her desk.

He glanced over his shoulder to see where the sound had come from, and Iz was there, standing by the door. He whipped

MEGAN O'RUSSELL

his head back toward the desk, but Iz's seat was now empty. Jacob turned slowly to look behind him again.

Iz smiled. "A party trick I know."

"But," Jacob sputtered, shaking his head. "But you were sitting. I was looking at you. How?"

Iz walked back to her seat at the desk. "Some might call it telekinesis. Some call us mutants, as the new popular media is inclined. But I prefer the terms *witch* and *wizard*. It is what we have been called historically, and it makes it seem far less likely that we will end up in a freak show. Or be captured by government agents and put into white rooms. Though, I'm not saying that isn't a possibility these days."

Jacob nodded again. White rooms, energy from inside him. It was too much.

"You can still go home, Jacob. I didn't want Emilia to retrieve you because I know how"—Iz stared into Jacob's eyes— "persuasive she has always been to you. If you stay here, we will shape you into a wonderful wizard. You will be able to do and see things that most can't even begin to imagine. But there are things you need to know. You're walking into a world on the brink of war, and unfortunately, the incident at Fairfield High may have made things worse."

"Incident? You mean what I did?"

"Yes." Iz nodded. "The *terrorist attack*."

"But it wasn't an attack. I didn't mean to do it. If it was even really me. Which I'm really not sure it was." Jacob started to feel fuzzy again.

"The human news says terrorist, and some members of Magickind seem to agree."

"What? It was an accident. I swear."

"I know, Jacob, but people see things the way they want to see them, not necessarily the way they are. There has been some"— Aunt Iz paused—"conflict of late within Magickind, particularly among wizards. Unfortunately, as the normal human population

26

expands, it leaves less room for the magical world to exist unde-tected. Some of us have started purchasing large tracts of land, adding to what was already owned by Magickind. You see, some of our people cannot co-exist with humans. Centaurs, fawns, fairies, mermen, griffins, dragons—"

Jacob leaned forward. "Are you serious? Dragons?"

"Jacob, dear"—Iz smiled—"if you can accept that you're a wizard, you need to accept that other legends are, in fact, real."

Jacob nodded slowly.

"Other wizards have started integrating more into society. Recent generations have even started to attend public schools. But there are also those who have taken a more radical approach." Iz paused, taking a slow sip of tea. "Attacking any humans who come near their homes and, in some cases, even killing them.

"Some wizards have recently gone so far as to attack humans who have in no way encroached on their territory. And I'm afraid your actions at your school yesterday"—she raised her hands as Jacob started to protest again—"however accidental they may have been, might be viewed along those lines. As a rebel act of terrorism, and the largest one we have seen in quite some time."

"But it was an accident," Jacob said. "I would never hurt anyone."

"And hopefully the rebels will understand that. But if they do view it as an attack, it may be the rallying point they have been waiting for. In which case, things could go very badly, very quickly. Ours is a delicate peace."

"So, what can I do?" Jacob asked, setting down his teacup harder than he had meant to. "How can I fix this?"

"There is nothing you can do to fix it, Jacob, but you could go back to Fairfield and never have to hear about any of this again. We would bind your powers. You could be normal."

Jacob thought for a moment. "And Emilia?"

"You would never see any of us again."

Jacob stared at Iz, trying to make sense of everything she was saying, but all he could see was a dragon and fire in his mind. But then Emilia's face replaced the horrible dragon.

"I'm staying. I want to stay. I want to be a wizard." Jacob stood, his gaze darting around the room as though a sign would appear that read *Being a wizard and staying with Emilia starts here*.

"All right." Iz held out a hand to stop his frantic search of the room.

"Is that why Emilia came to get me, because some"—Jacob swallowed, trying to say the word—"witches think I'm a terrorist?"

"No, we came to get you so quickly because we feared what other wizards might make of you if they got to you first." Iz stood, ending the conversation. "You don't need to be around people right now. You need time. Go rest. When you're ready, find Molly. She'll feed you."

Iz directed Jacob to his room. Up the main staircase, down a hall, and up a smaller staircase that led to the old servants' quarters, which had been declared the *Boys' Wing* by Connor.

Jacob shut himself into his assigned room on the top floor. The room was green, but not outrageously so. A large four-poster bed took up the center of the space with a green comforter that matched the green curtains and the green carpet. Small windows placed high in the walls peeked out through the sloped roof, looking out onto the trees that surrounded the house.

Someone had set a vase of fresh lilacs by the bed. The flowers filled the room with the subtle scent of a late afternoon. Jacob smiled. Emilia had left them for him. She knew he liked lilacs best, though he doubted she knew it was because the flowers reminded him of her.

Jacob wandered around his new bedroom. The carpet felt soft, even with his shoes on. He went into the bathroom. It was large, but manly. The shower was black granite from floor to ceiling with a sliding glass door. It was the sort of bathroom he had only ever seen in photographs.

He looked at himself in the mirror. He was pale. His eyes were red and swollen. And somewhere in this house, the girl he loved was either being yelled at by Iz or kissed by Dexter. His hands started to shake. Suddenly a hot shower seemed like the best idea in the world.

4

MADE TO BE BROKEN

*T*he sun was high in the sky when Jacob woke later that morning. He had put his dirty clothes back on after his shower since he couldn't find his bag. His brain ached, and he was starving. No one had told him where the kitchen was, so he wandered downstairs to look around.

The house was huge. Every surface had been polished to perfection. A crystal chandelier shone over the dining room table and large couches made room for a dozen people to sit in the living room.

Jacob wandered outside onto a stone veranda overlooking a sprawling garden filled with flowers and trees. Finally, he smelled something wonderful and found the kitchen.

He knocked.

"Come in, silly boy, and get your lunch. You look like a half-starved rat," Molly fussed as she examined him, clearly judging his lack of nutrition. A rather plump woman, Molly had the same bright red hair as her nephew and more freckles than anyone could ever count. "Eat, eat." She steered Jacob to sit down at her worktable where a plate waited for him.

Jacob started with the thick stew and a roll before he even bothered to look at his salad.

"That's a boy after my own heart." Molly laughed as she began to peel vegetables for the evening's dinner.

Jacob watched her for a few moments. "Molly, couldn't you just do that with magic?"

"Oh sure," she said. "*Pelloris.*" The carrot that had been in her hand ripped its skin off and placed itself on the cutting board. "But if you use magic all the time, it ruins the fun."

"Could I do that?" Jacob asked.

"Sure," Molly said with a smile, "but you'll need a few lessons first. We don't want you peeling yourself by accident. That would be a nasty one to fix."

"Could Emilia do that?" Jacob pointed to the perfectly peeled carrot and tried not to shudder at the thought of peeling himself. Would Aunt Iz be able to reattach his skin?

"She helps most days. But I'm afraid she's in a spot of trouble and will be in her room the rest of the day doing some rather difficult spell translations. Iz was not pleased with her running off in the middle of the night. Samuel would have been perfectly fine on his own." Molly moved on to the potatoes. "That girl is a strong-willed one. More stubborn than a pigheaded mule."

They sat in silence for a moment. Jacob's bread turned brown as it soaked up the juices from his stew.

"I should have known there was something different about her." Jacob shook his head. "She always seemed so much more, I don't know, real than the rest of us. So much more alive or connected." He pushed his plate away and grabbed a peeler to help Molly. "I should have noticed, or she should have told me."

"Don't you be judging her." Molly shook her knife at Jacob's nose. "It's not as though she didn't want to tell you. We have laws, you see. Magickind has been hiding for hundreds of years, and it hasn't been easy, mind. We've had to come up with rules and laws to govern us all. And one of the very first rules is keep the secret. Tell no one. If Emilia had told you, she would have been in for a world of trouble. Especially with the possibility of you joining us one day. That would have made it worse."

"What do you mean?"

"The minute someone displays any potential, if they are not a magical child already being raised by a magical family, all ties with anyone in the community must be immediately severed."

"But I never displayed any potential," Jacob said. "I never did any magic until yesterday."

"Do you remember the day we left?" Molly asked.

Jacob nodded. Nothing could make him forget that day.

"When Emilia fell, she broke her wrist. And you, Jacob"— Molly tossed him a potato to peel—"healed her. As soon as that happened, our laws forced us to leave Fairfield, and you, at once."

"But why?" Jacob asked angrily. "Wouldn't it have made more sense to teach me before I destroyed an entire school?"

Molly left her work to sit next to him. "My guess is the day you healed Emilia, you were terrified. Your blood was pumping, and you probably had a fair bit of adrenaline going, too. You did something beyond normal human capacity in an extremely stressful situation. That wouldn't necessarily make you a wizard. If Emilia had told you then and there all about witches and wizards and the rest, and you never showed another lick of magic after that, she would have broken the rules. That is why all contact had to be severed."

Jacob laughed and shook his head. "That's easy for you to say. But being left behind was—"

"Terrible," Molly finished for him, patting his arm. "I know. But don't go blaming anyone but the Council." Molly got up and returned to her pile of vegetables. "Iz said for you to go to her study as soon as you're ready. She'd like to get a start with you as quickly as possible."

Jacob got up to leave but stopped in the doorway. "What would they have done to her? If she had told me?"

"Stripped her of her powers," Molly said to the rhythm of her chopping. "And banished her from all contact with Magickind... forever. Makes you as good as dead if you ask me."

Jacob nodded slowly. "Thanks, Molly."

He drifted out of the kitchen, lost in thought. He took a wrong turn on his way to Iz's study and found himself in a large library. The walls were lined floor to ceiling with shelves of books. Desks were scattered around the room, each in a different state of disarray.

Connor and Dexter sat at their desks, engrossed in their work. Claire hummed loudly, rolling herself along on the ladder that allowed access to the higher shelves. There were empty desks in the library, too, and Jacob could tell which one was Emilia's, even though she wasn't there. Hers was the one with a vase of fresh flowers on it. He wondered if Dexter had brought them to her. Jacob shook his head and slipped away.

When he found Iz's study, her door waited open.

"Welcome to your first lesson." Aunt Iz clapped her hands delightedly as she rose from her armchair. "And let me say, Jacob, I am thrilled to be your teacher." She patted his cheek the same way she had when he was young. "Now, help an old lady to the garden. We're going to be practicing outside today. The weather is lovely, and I really don't want all the furniture bashed up again." She laughed merrily as they moved out into the hall and toward the veranda. Iz was not feeble in any way. In fact, she was more agile than most people half her age, but Jacob offered his arm anyway. "You would be amazed how often I have to redecorate."

"Couldn't you just fix the furniture with magic?" Jacob asked.

"If I did, I would still be stuck with the same furniture I had forty years ago." She smiled up at Jacob, her eyes twinkling. "And what fun would that be?"

They strolled past the stone veranda and down the path onto the lush lawn. Iz was right. It was a lovely day. Cherry blossoms dripped down from the trees, and the flowers balanced on the edge of full summer bloom. The garden was filled with so many trees, it looked more like a forest than any lawn Jacob had ever seen. There were beech trees and willows, giant evergreens and tiny saplings. But the most remarkable thing to Jacob was how alive everything felt.

The moisture in the air shot vitality through Jacob's veins. He could almost hear things growing within the earth. The green of the grass and trees was more vibrant than any he had ever seen. The flowers didn't look yellow or red or blue. They embodied what those colors were meant to be. And the smell...a thousand scents rolled into one that filled his lungs and made him feel thoroughly alive.

Aunt Iz stopped by a stone bench far enough down the path to hide the house from view. The bench sat in the center of a small clearing surrounded by trees and carpeted with wildflowers. She sat silently.

Jacob glanced up and down the path, searching for someone else who might be coming. "Why?" He brushed his fingers along the deep violet of a blooming iris. "Why is everything in this garden so much more alive than anything I've ever seen?"

"Because we sing to it," Aunt Iz answered simply.

Jacob didn't like singing. Music had never been an area in which he excelled. His music teacher in elementary school had written in his report card that he was lacking in musical ability and had difficulty matching pitch, but had a good work ethic. Trying and failing was not a quality he wanted to display on his first day with Iz.

"Even if the magic done on these grounds isn't specifically aimed at the flowers," Iz said, "they still come up to listen. This garden is wild and wonderful because as the earth feeds us the energy to do our magic, we also feed the earth."

"So, basically you make the flowers bloom?"

Aunt Iz looked up into the canopy of trees. "We don't make them. We supply the energy, and they do the growing. We nurture them and give them the strength they need to grow on their own. I suppose that's why I love my garden. It reminds me of my students."

Jacob followed Iz's gaze up to the treetops. The sunlight peered back at him through the leaves. As beautiful as the glittering emerald light was, he didn't see any magic.

"Now," Iz pondered aloud, "where to begin?" She leaned down and picked up a fallen leaf. She closed it in her hand and held it for a moment before blowing the leaf away.

The leaf didn't fall to the ground. It had folded itself like a paper airplane, and Iz's breath carried the plane up through the trees. The leaf slowly floated out of sight. "Magic is not some cosmic explosion. It is merely a manipulation of the world around you. There are some rules. Most are for safety's sake. And all have been broken at some point."

Jacob nodded his head. That sounded like physics. And physics he could do.

Aunt Iz continued, "The first thing we need to teach you is how to focus your mind. There is no point in teaching you spells if you are not focused enough to perform them without injuring yourself or others. Do you see this tree?" She stood and crossed to a tree Jacob hadn't noticed before.

Amidst the abundance of life in the garden, this one small sapling struggled to survive. It didn't have very many leaves and grew too crooked to be strong. Something so weak and deformed didn't belong in this place.

"Make it healthy." Aunt Iz patted Jacob's shoulder and headed back down the path to the house.

"What?" Jacob started after her.

She turned him around and pushed him back to the clearing.

"But how?" he said. "I'm really sorry, Aunt Iz, but I think that tree is doomed."

"Tell me when it's green," Aunt Iz called over her shoulder.

Jacob looked at the sad little tree. "You have got to be kidding me."

5

SOUNDS IN THE NIGHT

*H*e closed his eyes and took a deep breath. "All right," Jacob said to himself with much more confidence than he felt. "I can totally do this. She wouldn't assign me an impossible task." But he couldn't quite figure out how to go about saving the tree.

It needed to make chlorophyll, which required light, water, and air. Maybe he could find a watering can and some fertilizer. He had done plenty of yard work back home whenever money ran out.

Samuel had actually been the one who taught him how to take care of plants when the Grays still lived in Fairfield. Samuel had never used magic for gardening. At least Jacob didn't think so. Jacob pushed his palms into his eyes and rubbed hard.

"I need to rethink my entire childhood. There must have been magic in Emilia's house. I was just too stupid to notice."

Maybe the tree had a bug problem. But he doubted the answer was so dull. He searched the clearing for a clue, a sign of some sort, but found nothing. Finally, after several minutes of fruitless scouring of the grass, he sat cross-legged on the ground and stared at the poor tree.

Hours passed. Jacob tried asking the tree for suggestions. The tree was unhelpful. Jacob's limbs ached from sitting for so long, so he started pacing in wide circles around the tree. When his feet got tired, Jacob tried closing his eyes and picturing the tree strong and healthy. Again he tried asking the tree what would make it feel better. But it was no good. He had no idea how to heal a tree by magic.

In an act of sheer desperation, he tried singing to the tree. His off-key rendition of *I've Been Working on the Railroad* did nothing.

Finally, when the sun had begun making its way back down, a voice carried up the path calling him in for the night.

Claire waited for him on the veranda, smiling mischievously. "Good first day?" she asked as she led Jacob back into the house.

"Yeah." Jacob tried to sound at least a little cheerful.

"Liar." Claire's extremely blond left eyebrow climbed very high on her forehead. "Don't worry. I did tons of magic by accident before I came here, and it still took me forever to be able to do anything I actually wanted to do. You're not stupid. It's just hard."

"Thanks, Claire," Jacob said, feeling a little better. Voices drifted from the dining room, and he stopped Claire right before they walked in. "But could you do me a favor?"

"Don't tell Dexter you're having trouble?" Claire smirked. "Sure." She walked into the dining room, giggling.

"Jacob." Professor Eames stood up at one end of the table. "Please choose a seat."

Jacob looked around the table. There was an open seat next to Samuel and one next to Dexter.

Dexter looked at Jacob and nodded.

Jacob clenched his fists and took a breath before sitting next to Samuel, where he would be less likely to cause a major incident. Like a falling chandelier.

The entire household was at the table, except for Emilia. She was probably still stuck in her room.

"Greens first," Aunt Iz said to Connor from her seat at the head of the table.

"Yes, ma'am." Connor reluctantly replaced the dish of cheese-smothered potatoes.

"Professor Eames," Dexter said after placing a large portion of salad onto his plate, "I read an article on the Siren Theory and its implications in the ability of wizards to impose paradoxical travel on those around them, as well as its possible connection to the 1892 smugglers' brigade disappearance. I was wondering if you might have any insight."

The conversation flowed like dry mud during dinner. Professor Eames and Dexter engaged in a lively discussion, with Aunt Iz inserting important concepts Jacob didn't understand. Molly and Samuel joined in occasionally, and Claire and Connor both seemed to follow along, nodding in all the right places. Jacob felt lost and in way over his head. As dinner came to an end, everyone helped bring the dishes to the kitchen before going to the living room.

Jacob took a seat on a comfy couch off to the side, and Dexter followed him.

"Did you enjoy dinner?" Dexter sat on the arm of the couch Jacob had chosen. "I always look forward to our dinner discussions. They are so enlightening. Did you enjoy the subject tonight?"

"Sure." Jacob forced a smile. "But I'm really wiped, so I'm gonna go."

He stood and walked out of the room, barely pausing to wave to Aunt Iz and Samuel, who were deep in conversation at a small table in the corner.

Dexter must have known he didn't understand a damn thing they'd said at dinner. Jacob climbed the stairs to his room, trying not to give in to the temptation to give one of the stairs a good kick. A broken toe wouldn't make him feel much better. He was too tired to be social anyway. Emilia was still banished to her room, and she was the only one he really wanted to talk to.

Jacob found his room and slammed the door. He winced at the sound, hoping no one downstairs had heard. Jacob tried lying on his bed, but he couldn't seem to breathe. This was too much, far too much to deal with in one day. His father was dead, he had left the only home he had ever known, and he was a wizard.

He rolled onto his back and rubbed his face with both hands. Emilia was back. She was a witch. She had come back because he was a wizard. He knew he should be grieving. He should be scared. He had essentially dropped out of high school. He didn't know when he would be going back to Fairfield High. Or if.

Jacob pressed the heels of his hands hard into his eyes. He needed air.

High school dropout, orphan, incompetent wizard.

Jacob's bedroom windows were open, wafting in the cool evening breeze. He followed the fresh air to the window and squeezed himself through onto the slanting shingles of the roof. He sat, breathing deeply and trying to muddle through the last thirty-six hours of his life. Stars emerged from the darkness. Even though Fairfield was a small city, it still didn't have as many stars as Jacob could see from here. The trees rustled as unseen creatures prowled through the night. He closed his eyes, trying to imagine centaurs pacing through the woods.

The centaurs screamed at him, calling him a terrorist. Jacob's eyes snapped open when one of the centaurs threw a spear at him. He shook the fantasy from his mind and tried to focus on the real world around him. His mind was too jumbled right now to let it wander. He listened again to the sounds of the night. There was a new noise, a strange noise, and it was on the roof. A scraping sound, like claws pulling across the shingles, moving closer. He looked over and froze. Someone was coming toward him, not clawing the roof, but walking on the air.

6

THE ORPHANED GRAY

*F*or a moment, panic flooded Jacob's chest, but even in the pale moonlight he recognized Emilia. She wore a nightgown and walked very slowly.

Jacob rubbed his eyes to be sure he wasn't hallucinating. But when he opened them, Emilia was still moving toward him. It looked like she was walking on stones trying to cross a creek without getting wet. A *scrape* punctuated each step as shingles pulled themselves off the roof and floated in the air for Emilia to walk on. As she passed, they would *rasp* themselves back into place, leaving no sign they had ever moved at all. Jacob shook his head in amazement.

"Kind of cool, huh?" Emilia stood on two shingles that hovered in the air, waiting for her to take the next step.

Jacob nodded, trying not to look shocked by her entrance.

"How are you?" Emilia stepped onto the roof and sat down beside him as though she hadn't done anything abnormal. The two shingles she had been standing on scraped themselves back into their usual place.

"It's been a little crazy."

They sat in silence for a moment.

"Oh, here." Jacob reached into his pocket and pulled out a little pouch. Just a bit of fabric and some string. He'd made it himself to hold the necklace Emilia had left with him. Jacob always carried the pouch with him. He had every day since she'd left. He took Emilia's hand and slid the necklace from the pouch onto her palm.

Emilia's eyes lit up. "You still have it." She turned the sapphire pendant over in her hand before sliding the long chain around her neck. "Thank you, Jacob. Thank you for keeping it safe for me."

Her smile stole his breath away.

"No problem." He stared at his worn shoes. Silence overtook them again. A thousand things Jacob had wanted to say to her over the last four years raced through his mind. Things about his life and school and wanting to go to college. But now, with Emilia sitting right next to him, only one question came out. "Why did you leave it with me anyway?" Jacob asked, his voice sounding gruffer than he had meant it to.

"So you would know I was coming back," Emilia said. "You knew this was the only thing I had from my mother. You knew I would never abandon it, just like I would never abandon you. Leaving you like that was a horrible thing to do, but I didn't have a choice. I couldn't explain. I wasn't allowed to. I wasn't even supposed to say goodbye. But I wanted you to know I was coming back, even if you didn't know why I had to leave."

She paused, but he couldn't think of anything to say.

"Jacob, it was the best promise I could make."

"Why does the necklace matter to you?" Jacob looked Emilia in the eye, searching for a truth he could actually understand. "Was it even your mother's?"

"I think it was," she said. "I really don't know."

"How can you not know?"

"I always told you my mother died when I was little, and Aunt Iz was my only relative," Emilia said. "That's not really the truth.

Someone left me on the doorstep here with a note and this necklace when I was only a few days old." Emilia looked down at the sapphire pendant. Delicate veins of silver held the deep blue teardrop stone in place. "Aunt Iz decided she might as well keep me since someone had left me specifically for her, especially since it seemed I would turn out to be a witch.

"There was no point in trying to find me a normal family if she would just have to come take me back in a few years anyway. I guess the necklace must have been my mother's since she left it with me. At least I assume my mother left me. I don't know who else could have." Emilia spun the pendant between her fingers. The sapphire caught the moonlight and sparkled brighter than it had during the four years Jacob had kept it for her.

"Aunt Iz didn't mind someone leaving a baby on her doorstep?" Jacob asked.

"Iz would never turn anyone away. Especially not a cute little baby."

It was odd to Jacob that Emilia didn't seem bothered by this. That it was all right her mother had abandoned her on someone's doorstep.

"It's okay." Jacob took Emilia's hand in his. His heart caught in his chest, and he quickly let go. "I get why you wouldn't want to tell me your mom left you."

"I'm sorry I never told you. It just seemed too strange. If you didn't know my mother was a witch, it wouldn't make sense for her to leave me with Aunt Iz."

Jacob shook his head. "I know what it's like to have family stuff you don't want to talk about."

"Jacob, it's not like that. I would tell you anything. I trust you more than anyone else. *Dead* is easier than *missing witch*, that's all." She laughed a little.

Jacob couldn't really understand why.

"Did you ever try to find her?" he asked.

"She could find me if she wanted to. I'm still here."

"I'm sorry."

"Don't be," Emilia said. "I got lucky. I got Iz."

"Why were you allowed to stay?" He didn't want to find a hole in her story. Didn't want another reason to be angry.

"The note Aunt Iz found with me said *Care for my Emilia. She will be one of us.*"

"But if proof is necessary—"

"Exactly. Proof of ancestry wasn't possible, so Aunt Iz called a Council meeting. She cared for me in the week before the gathering could take place. Of course, she just had to decorate a nursery, and she bought me a mobile with stars on it. Apparently, I didn't like when the mobile stopped turning, because I started turning the stars myself with magic. Aunt Iz wrote to the Council of Elders and told them they didn't need to bother with the meeting. And that was it. I had shown I was a witch, so it was completely within the rules for her to keep me."

Emilia smiled at Jacob. Leaves and twigs from the roof rose above their heads and slowly started to circle around them like a solar system. All the objects rotated perfectly along their orbits with Emilia as their sun. "Still one of my favorite tricks."

"How does it work?" He waved his hand at the swirling leaves.

"You're not supposed to cheat." Emilia hugged her knees closer to her chest. "And my helping you would definitely qualify as cheating."

"But I don't understand. Half-dead trees don't just get better." Jacob yanked a hand through his hair. "That's not how things work."

Emilia reached up and took his hand. She pulled a leaf from the air and placed it in his palm.

"Yes," she said. "That is exactly how it works." She smiled and the leaf turned a vibrant shade of green, as bright as any other in the garden. "That is how it works for me and for you, Jacob. You have to leave behind all of the rules you thought existed. Because this"—she looked up at her halo of leaves—"is real, and you can be a part of this world. I know you can. You belong here with us."

Jacob wondered if *us* included Dexter. "Would you have come back for me if I couldn't do magic? Would it have bothered you to never see me again?"

"Of course." Tears glistened in the corners of her eyes. "Of course I would have come back for you. I had to wait. There are rules—"

"Who cares about the rules?" Jacob snapped, anger creeping back into his voice. "You were my best friend. I needed you, and you weren't there."

"I know." Tears streamed freely down her face. "I've tried a million times to think of another way, but the Council would never allow it. I'm sorry. I'm so sorry I left you all alone."

"I always wondered why Iz didn't take me. I mean, if your mother died and she took you. But she never offered to take me. She fed me, bought me shoes, took me to the doctor, but never wanted me to live with you."

"I asked her." Emilia stared out over the trees. "I wanted her to take you, too. You would have been happy with us. But she said no. It wouldn't have been safe if you lived with us. Eventually, you would have figured out we were witches, and then we would all have been in trouble. So I started wishing for you to be a wizard. Then I finally got my wish, and we had to leave you behind completely."

Jacob brushed her tears away with his thumb. It didn't matter how much he hurt. He never wanted to see Emilia cry. "But you came back," he said. "I'm here now, and you won't have to leave me behind again."

"I told them I had to come and get you myself." Emilia turned away from Jacob and looked back out into the night. "Because if I didn't, you would never have forgiven me."

Jacob lay back on the roof and gazed at the stars as Emilia's solar system circled around them.

7

THE LIFE OF A TREE

*J*acob woke up early the next morning. The sun peered through his window, shining into his eyes. But he didn't open them. If he hadn't dreamt the last forty-eight hours of his life, then he was at Aunt Iz's house, he was a wizard brought here to be trained, Emilia had come back for him because his father was dead, he had destroyed his school, and he was suspected of being a terrorist. And Emilia had a boyfriend who had no problem kissing her in front of the entire family. Jacob's new family.

Jacob lay in bed, trying not to think about real or not real. As his mind started to clear, he realized the bedsprings weren't poking him. He moved his foot and his toes brushed along soft sheets made of some kind of fabric he had definitely never slept in before.

He opened his eyes and found himself in the green room. He couldn't have slept for more than a few hours, and yet he was wide awake. Rolling quickly out of bed, Jacob strode to the bathroom and studied himself in the mirror. He still looked the same as he always had. More tired maybe, but the same.

"I am a wizard," Jacob said firmly to himself. "I am Jacob

Evans, and I am a wizard." It still didn't sound right. "Hi, I'm Jacob, and I'm a wizard. I've been a wizard for two days now." Jacob laughed. The sound bounced around the room.

He stepped into the shower, turned the water on as hot as he could stand, and pressed his forehead to the cold granite wall. This new life was going to take some getting used to.

When he finished showering, Jacob went to the closet to look for his bag, assuming it must have made it to his room by now. But the closet was filled with clothes Jacob had never seen before. A note was stuck on the front of the clothes that read *Compliments of Claire.*

Everything in the closet was clearly brand new, but all of the tags had been removed. The clothes were very stylish and expensive looking. Suddenly Claire's excitement at his arrival made perfect sense. She had wanted the excuse to go shopping. As he dug for his bag in the bottom of the closet, he found another note.

Took your clothes, so you'll have to wear these.

Kisses,

Claire

Jacob scrunched the note in his hand and chose the least expensive-looking thing he could find: a pair of jeans and a soft red T-shirt. The outfit probably cost more money than he usually spent on food in a month. It fit him perfectly. Had Claire somehow measured him magically, or was she just that good at shopping? As soon as he stepped into the hall, he was greeted by the smell of Molly's delicious cooking wafting up the stairs.

He paused on the landing. For the first time in a very long time, he had a roof with no leaks, clothes that fit, and a hot breakfast waiting for him downstairs. His life may have been turned upside down, but things were definitely looking up.

Jacob was surprised to find Claire and Connor already in the living room.

"Breakfast will be ready in a bit." Connor glanced up from his book. "You can sit with us to wait if you'd like."

Jacob sat on the massive, rust-colored couch in the center of the room. Connor smiled at him but apparently didn't feel the need to fill the silence. Claire, however, muttered under her breath while staring very intently at her feet.

Jacob watched for a few moments until his curiosity got the better of him. "What are you doing?"

Claire didn't respond, so Connor answered for her. "She obsesses over her nails."

Jacob leaned forward to look.

"I am thinking very deep and important thoughts," Claire retorted while changing the shade of pink polish on her toes to be slightly pinker with a few muttered words.

"Right." Jacob leaned back on the couch.

"So, big day for you, huh?" Claire said, seemingly satisfied with her pedicure.

"Claire," Connor said.

"What?" Claire cocked her head to one side with the look of a confused puppy. "He just got thrown into the magical crazy pot. You grew up being a wizard. You don't get it. I know what it's like to figure out this freak stuff is for real." She turned to Jacob. "When they took me from my home when I was seven, they told me fairies were real and I was destined to be something more, and not to screw up because MAGI would come after me. That sort of thing really messes with your head."

"MAGI?" Jacob asked.

"Magical Agency for the Gathering of Intelligence," Connor said. "The Council of Elders created MAGI to deal with safety, secrecy, and law enforcement issues. They run everything. Even Spellnet." At the confused look on Jacob's face, Connor added, "Spellnet is a computer program. Magic leaves very distinctive energy waves, and MAGI set up a system to monitor those energy waves by satellite. It's a huge organization. And the satellites' nets cover the entire globe."

"Wizards use computers?" Jacob asked.

Connor nodded. "Keeping tabs on all the wizards in the United States got a lot easier when MAGI switched from paper files to a computer database."

"Right."

"Only problem is you can't do too much magic near electronics. One too many spells with your cellphone in your pocket, and the phone gets fried. It happens to Dexter all the time. He always has his phone on him. MAGI agents have crazy rules for what they can do in headquarters. They use human locks on the doors and firewalls on the computers."

"There is nothing wrong with a little human hacking," Claire snapped.

Connor hid his face in his book.

"And," Claire continued, "all the MAGI databases and Spellnet are funded by normal people who buy MAGI inventions. MAGI takes magical concepts and converts them into technology. Which is why Iz has such nice things. But she shares the wealth. She bought the Graylock Preserve so the centaurs could have more land. And she sends money wherever it's needed. She just bought a bunch of land in Africa, but she won't let me visit." Claire sulked, picking up her polish bottle and starting on her fingernails.

"Why Africa?" Jacob asked.

"Dragons. They only live in Africa. We don't keep them in America anymore," Claire said.

"Why?"

"They're lizards. They like the desert," said a sarcastic voice from behind Jacob's shoulder.

Jacob turned to see Dexter leaning against the doorframe, grinning as if dragons being in the desert should have been common sense to a kindergartener.

"They were hunted to near extinction in New Mexico and Texas," Dexter said. "They used to love Death Valley, but now there are too many tourists. So the remaining dragons were sent to Africa. There's more space there. The dragons were pushed out of their rightful territory by humans. That's why the rebels have named themselves the Dragons. In honor of the true kings of nature that were forced into hiding."

Connor shot Dexter a look that clearly said *shut up*.

The room fell silent for a moment.

"And these Dragons are saying I attacked my school?" Jacob tried to put the pieces together. "How did you guys know what happened at the school was caused by me?"

"MAGI Trackers." Connor turned back to Jacob. "The Council has a team that monitors large spikes in magic on Spellnet. They have a grid system of the whole world, and if anything spikes it, they go investigate. Luckily, Ms. Gray has friends on the tracker team. They tipped her off so we could get to you first. She told them your area was of special interest to her."

"What would've happened if you hadn't gotten to me?"

"We think the Dragons have someone inside the tracker team, too, because lately they've been getting to some of the new ones first," Claire said.

"Then what?"

"We don't really hear about anyone once they're with the rebels," Dexter said. "Some say they kill them. But in my opinion, they train them."

"For what?"

"Who knows?" Connor cut in with another hard look at Dexter. "But I'm sure it's not good for us." The room turned to ice as Dexter and Connor glared at each other. "We watch, and they watch. It's just a matter of who gets there first."

"How about werewolves?" Jacob asked, more to break the tension than because he actually wanted an answer.

"Werewolfism is a rabies-like disease," Professor Eames said as he entered the living room. "The last known case was in 1954. It is believed the disease has been eradicated, but there are frequent rumors of the existence of werewolf colonies."

"In my research, werewolfism is spread through insect bites." Claire picked up her bright pink computer from the floor.

"Have you been conducting research, Claire?" the professor asked, smiling.

"Yes. The werewolf disease is actually spread through the bite and subsequent attachment of lunaticks." Claire looked around. "Get it? Luna-ticks, like the moon, and crazy people. No? Emilia thought it was funny."

"I believe breakfast is ready." The professor chuckled as he led the way to the dining room.

8

WHERE TO BEGIN?

*B*reakfast was wonderful. Eggs, bacon, sausage, and fruit. Molly kept loading double portions of everything onto Jacob's plate, while keeping up a running commentary on how thin he was and how a growing boy needed a sturdy breakfast. Jacob was so full he thought he might not need to eat for days. Molly, however, was still trying to put more food on his plate when the professor stood up and said, "Jacob, I believe it is time for our lesson."

The professor led Jacob down the hall to his private study. Jacob had expected the room to look exciting, filled with cauldrons or strange gadgets, but it looked like a normal elderly gentleman's library. He was surprised to find many of the book titles were familiar to him and seemed not at all magical. The professor had *The Complete Works of William Shakespeare* and several volumes of Charles Dickens. There was *Walden* by Thoreau, as well as large sections on physics and astronomy.

There were, however, several unusual-looking volumes on the desk. One rather old and exceedingly large volume lay open. The book wasn't ancient, but more like a well-worn textbook.

There were notes in the margins and creases in the binding where some pages had been turned too many times.

"Now, Jacob, where to begin?" Professor Eames asked as he seated himself behind his desk.

Jacob stared at the professor, hoping he wasn't expected to answer. His mind was still half wondering if a woodland fairy was going to be given the breakfast leftovers by Molly.

The professor leafed through a file on his desk. "Magic is a very complicated and dangerous endeavor. Isadora will teach you how to find the power within yourself. I will teach you how not to harm yourself or others. And I am afraid my lessons will be rather more tedious. You must learn the history of our kind, the language of magic, and the current status of Magickind around the world. Although"—Professor Eames ran his finger down a sheet of paper and tapped the bottom. He smiled at Jacob, his face creasing in well-worn wrinkles—"according to the school records MAGI pulled for you, you are an exemplary student. Fairfield High School, by the way, thinks you have transferred to a private learning institution, which is as close to the truth as is necessary."

Jacob nodded, unsure what the appropriate response would be.

Professor Eames reached under his desk and pulled out three books, the largest of which was an identical but less worn copy of the open volume on the desk. "These three books hold the majority of our magical knowledge. The *Compendium* is a written account of our history and laws, and it defines the lines between good and bad magic." Professor Eames placed a black leather book on the table. "*ATLAS*, or *Acknowledged Territories, Lands, and Societies*, maps out which groups live where, what the defined boundaries are between territories, and contains a breakdown of Wizarding Clans and magical species." *ATLAS* was a large, flat book with a green cover.

"*Lingua Veneficium* is a record of spells, complete with instructions on how to perform the incantations." This was the large red book like the one lying open on the desk. "These books are only owned by wizards, and the penalty for allowing any of these volumes to fall into non-wizard hands is very steep. The most important thing is to keep the secret."

Jacob picked up *Lingua Veneficium*, opened it, and scanned the text. "These spells are based in Latin. I recognize the roots."

"I see your academic prowess has not been overestimated." A smile lit Professor Eames' face. "The spells are based in Latin. Latin is a common language that is rarely spoken. It is useful to us for the same reason it is useful to scientists. We call the language used in spells the *Lingua Magnifica*."

"So, is there something special about Latin?" Jacob flipped through his new textbook. His magical textbook. "Did magic originate with that language?"

"You don't need words for magic. Words simply make it easier for you to focus your energy. You can think *fire* and the candle may light, but so might the curtains, or the cat. And I am rather fond of that poor little cat." Eames chuckled at his own joke.

Jacob laughed feebly.

"Some words that have been used for hundreds or even thousands of years are now magical," Professor Eames said, "but only because of the magic wizards have poured into them."

As the professor spoke, Jacob pictured each of the words floating out of his mouth as a spell bursting with light.

"So if I say"—Jacob paused, looking for a word in his book —"*umbrafere*, I'll turn into a shadow?"

The professor grinned. "If you were focusing your magic behind it, yes, but since you have yet to master that, no. Nothing would happen. The power comes from the mind itself. Exacting your will on the world around you. We can change objects because deep down they are all matter. The universe doesn't care what form the matter takes. As long as you do not try to create or destroy matter, really it's all the same. All of the spoken spells and wands or talismans are just ways of focusing your energy. It's not the talisman that is important. It is the power of the wizard behind the talisman."

"Talisman?" Jacob's brows knit together. He pictured himself trying to heal the tree with a life-sized crystal skull.

The professor rested his chin on his hands. "Think of magic as electricity. The human body can conduct small amounts of electricity without sustaining physical damage. But if you send enough volts through the body, a human will die. A wizard can conduct a small amount of magic, but if the energy is too great, death is the inevitable result. The purpose of a talisman is to help you focus the energy away from your body and into a chosen external object to avoid overloading your system.

"A talisman isn't necessary for minor spells, but any major spell attempted without a talisman could very easily prove fatal. And a talisman can be anything, but it is better if you feel a connection to it. It can be something you find, create, or inherit. And it will have no magical significance until you start to use it. Eventually, as you send more magic through your chosen object, it will begin to retain some of your magic. It will remember how magic works and will eventually increase your strength and power."

"So," Jacob said, picking up a pen that was sitting next to him, "basically what you're saying is I could use this as a talisman?"

"In theory, yes. But it probably won't work very well. To use the electricity metaphor, it may not be the right conductor for you. And if you use it once and afterward leave it behind, and then use a stick once and leave it behind, you'll never build any power in your talisman or become truly comfortable with it."

"How do you know what talisman is right for you?"

"You will know when it comes to you. I fashioned my wand from a broken fence post on my family's farm the day I decided I needed to leave them a very long time ago. Emilia was given a ring on her seventh birthday that she uses. She used her necklace until she left it behind with you. Samuel has a staff. He's always loved being outdoors, and he says a good sturdy staff is more useful than just about anything else. And, if worse comes to worst, he can always bash someone on the head with it."

"Hmm," was all Jacob could manage. He imagined himself in the grocery store carrying a giant staff, king of the frozen food section.

Professor Eames didn't seem to notice Jacob's mind wandering. "Dexter has two talismans actually, which, while still functional, is not really necessary, but his wrist cuffs were heirlooms. You should set your mind to finding a talisman as quickly as possible. I am afraid you must be on the educational fast track, if you'll forgive the term."

"Why?"

The professor examined his wrinkled hands for a moment. "Isadora informed you of the rebel situation, did she not? If the Council does view you as a threat to Magickind, either because you are in league with these self-styled Dragons or because you are uncontrollable, then you may not be allowed to stay with us. The Council would either bind your powers or send you to the Academy."

"The Academy?"

"Most magical families either pass down the knowledge themselves, or in a case where a parent wants a higher magical education for their child, they are sent to professors, such as myself, for an apprenticeship. That is why Dexter is here. He and Emilia have both been my apprentices for a few years now.

"Some children born into families where no one else has magical abilities are also sent to professors for education, like Claire. In the case of students who do not have a family to foster them as we have fostered Claire, or who are too difficult to control, they are sent to the Academy, the only formal magical school in America. It is not the most pleasant place, and I can assure you, you will receive a much better education here."

"Right." Jacob pictured cold, grey walls and lines of cots in vast dormitories. He definitely did not want to be sent to some institution, and he would not leave Emilia. "Fast track it is."

"Then let us begin!" Professor Eames exclaimed.

Jacob spent the rest of the day in the study with the professor, though Professor Eames never asked him to do any magic. They spent most of the time working on spell phrasing.

The professor insisted Jacob not try any magic until he had succeeded in completing Aunt Iz's task. As the hours passed, Jacob wanted to scream that if he wasn't to do magic until the tree was healthy, he might as well go pack his bag for the Academy now. But would the Academy even take him? Still, Professor Eames seemed perfectly content to work on pronunciation.

When there was only a half hour until dinner, the professor sent Jacob away, instructing him to read some of *Lingua Veneficium* that night.

Jacob dropped his books in his room and went to find Emilia, wanting to tell her everything Professor Eames had told him. He went down the old servants' staircase into the main body of the house, where the bedrooms had taller ceilings and bigger closets. Emilia, Claire, Iz, and Molly all lived on the second floor of the house in the Ladies' Wing. Down here, portraits lined the hall, hanging between oversized windows. Jacob preferred his cozy attic room. Sleeping with a chandelier would have felt too much like living in a museum.

Jacob wandered down the wide and carpeted hallway. He didn't know where to find Emilia's room. He was about to call out for her when he heard raised voices down the corridor. He crept forward, not wanting to disturb anyone, before realizing the voices belonged to Dexter and Emilia.

"You went to see him last night, didn't you?" Dexter's voice slipped through the crack under the door.

"Yes," Emilia answered in a very matter-of-fact tone.

"What were you doing?" Dexter demanded.

"Talking, Dex. Just talking." Jacob could tell from the tone of her voice she was tense. Dexter was treading on thin ice. "I used to go over to his house every night, and we would talk, just like last night. His life has fallen apart. He lost his father, found out he's a wizard...he's my best friend, and he needs me."

Dexter snorted.

"What?" Emilia asked. "What is your problem with him? He's my friend. Can't you at least try to be nice to him?"

"No," Dexter said flatly, "because he shouldn't be here."

Angry footsteps pounded toward Jacob.

"Em, wait. Look, I know he's been through a lot. But he should go to the Academy."

Jacob heard Emilia growl. He knew that growl. It meant Dexter was screwed. Apparently, Dexter sensed the danger as well.

"No, listen to me," Dexter said. "He shouldn't be here. Not after what he did to that school. He should be someplace more controlled."

More footsteps resonated through the door as Emilia tried again to leave. Dexter's heavier footfalls shook the floor as he chased after her.

"He should be with more people like us. See what our world is really like."

"But he's my friend," Emilia said.

"That's not all he wants."

There was silence. Jacob's heart pounded so hard he could hear it.

Dexter spoke again. "You know I'm right."

Seconds ticked past as Jacob held his breath, waiting for her response.

"I love you, Emilia," Dexter said. "And I trust you. But don't expect me to be happy he's here. I hope he knows I will fight to keep you."

For a moment, everything was quiet, as though the entire world were waiting for Emilia to say something. Suddenly, heavy footsteps moved toward him. Jacob barely had time to dart through an open door across the hall and hide before Dexter stalked past. Jacob pressed himself against the wall and waited to be sure Dexter was gone.

So Emilia knew. She knew he was in love with her. But she hadn't told Dexter she would never be interested in Jacob, hadn't said he could never be anything more than a childhood friend.

Jacob smiled to himself. He might have a chance.

He listened carefully as a minute ticked past, then peered around the corner to make sure the hall was empty before creeping down to the dining room. He could talk to Emilia later. The last thing he wanted to do right now was distract her from how pissed off she was at Dexter. He sat down to dinner, determined to be as nice to Dexter as humanly, or rather, wizardly possible. Let Emilia decide who was the better man.

9

GREEN

*J*acob propped all his pillows at the head of his bed and settled in to do his reading in *Lingua Veneficium*. The professor had only told him to familiarize himself with the format of the spells, not assigned specific chapters for reading. The book didn't seem to have chapters anyway. Nor was it in alphabetical order, at least not by spell wording or English translation. Rather, the book seemed to be categorized by desired spell results. Though there were no section headings.

Jacob flipped to a page where each of the spells seemed to involve lifting. *Elevare* was a levitation spell designed to lift physical objects. And *cantus relovare* was used to lift simple curses.

All of the spells included their wording, or for more complex spells, the necessary incantation, but none actually said how the magic part was supposed to work.

Inluminaquio included a note about only being able to be performed under a full moon. *Spessenatura* was done by drawing out the essence of the object the wizard desired to copy, thus the talisman had to be in contact with said object.

Jacob slammed the book shut and was sorely tempted to chuck it across the room. He needed to be on the fast track. To prove he should be here. To prove he was good enough for Emilia. And reading through a bunch of spells wasn't helping.

He rubbed his eyes, trying to push the temptation of sleep from his mind, and looked out the window. The treetops swayed in the gentle breeze, shifting the stars in and out of view. The tree was the key.

Jacob got out of bed and picked up his *Lingua Veneficium*. He opened his door quietly and crept into the hall. He paused to listen but didn't hear anyone moving about the house. No one had said he had to stay inside at night, but he assumed Iz wouldn't appreciate his going out to the garden at one in the morning.

Nothing stirred but the swaying trees as he slipped out the veranda doors and onto the garden path. The moon was bright, and he easily found his way to the frail little tree.

Again he tried sitting in front of the tree, willing it to be healthy. He tried asking the tree nicely. He even tried saying a few of the spells he'd found in his book. *"Adfirmare. Sanavire. Alescere!"* He was sure he had the pronunciation right, but nothing worked.

Jacob was about to go back to the house and look through the shelves of books in the library to find a clue. Those books had to have something in them about dying plants.

He was tired, so tired, but determined to finish this.

Trying to decide what to look up when he got back to the house, he closed his eyes and laid his hand on the thin trunk of the tree. Suddenly, a flash of something strange flared before him, like a feeble light flickering from the center of the tree. Jacob yanked his hand away. He opened his eyes and examined the sapling.

The tiny trunk remained bent, and the leaves withering and frail. Jacob carefully placed his hand back on the tree and closed his eyes. There it was, the light in the center of the tree again, but he was prepared this time and didn't shy away.

Ever so slowly, he became aware of another light, an energy within himself, but it burned brighter and stronger than the light in the tree. He took a breath and felt the core of energy burn hotter with the flow of air, as though a bed of hot embers were living under his lungs, feeding on the oxygen they pulled in. Tentatively, almost instinctively, Jacob pushed a little energy out into his hand.

In an instant, the light connected with the tree, as if the spark within his body and within the tree were magnets drawn together. The energy flowed out of his body, but it didn't feel like he was losing anything. There seemed to be a source inside him so vast the amount of energy he poured into the tree was insignificant. Or else he had a limitless supply.

The light in the tree became stronger and brighter. Then gently, very gently, he released the connection. For a moment, he was afraid the tree would fade. He didn't want to open his eyes and find the tree was still sickly, or worse, dead.

But when he opened his eyes, the tree had bloomed. It was still small, but the branches were covered in new green leaves. The tree emanated life, just like the rest of the garden. Jacob stared, amazed at what he had done.

Magic. He had done magic.

Exhaustion took over his body, weighing down his arm. He couldn't help laughing as he lay back on the grass.

"Yet another redefinition of impossible."

There was a snap from the tree above him, and a single branch fell, smacking him hard on the face. Jacob sat up, rubbing the sore spot on his nose. A stick lay in the grass next to him, about a foot long and almost perfectly straight. He stared for a moment. Had the tree meant to hit him? Maybe the tree was angry because it hadn't wanted to be healed. Was there such a thing as a suicidal tree?

He held the stick up to the tree. "You want this back?" he asked, only half joking.

Then the moonlight peeked through the trees, shining down on Jacob. The stick in his hand shimmered in the pale light. It was thick on one end and slowly tapered to a point on the other. The thicker end seemed to fit perfectly in his hand, with a slight groove for his first finger to nestle in. There were no knots or imperfections, and the wood was so smooth it looked almost polished.

It was a wand. His wand. His talisman.

Jacob patted the tree as he got up to go to bed. "Thank you." And proudly carrying his wand, he followed the moonlit path back to the house.

~

*B*right stars filled the night, and a cool spring breeze whispered through the trees. Emilia shivered, and Dexter wrapped his arm around her, leading her deeper into the woods. Into the wilder part of the garden where no one would be able to see them from the path.

Emilia peered through the dense shadows. She could have sworn she'd heard footsteps on the path a minute ago. A rustling shook the bushes. Emilia gasped as a red fox darted past them.

"Shh," Dexter whispered. "He won't hurt you. You're with me." He smiled and kissed her on the forehead.

"Dexter, what are we doing out here?" Emilia pulled away.

"I wanted some time alone with you." Dexter drew Emilia farther into the trees.

"Dex—"

"No arguing, Emilia," Dexter cut her off, kissing her hair. "I wanted to tell you I'm sorry for our fight this afternoon."

"Thank you." She rested her head on his shoulder, enjoying the softness of his shirt on her face. "But we aren't allowed to be out here like this. If Aunt Iz finds out, she'll kill us. Possibly literally."

Dexter lifted her face and looked into her eyes. "You were on the roof with Jacob last night." He tucked her hair behind her ear.

"Dex, that's different."

Dexter kissed her. His mouth soft but possessive. "Yes," he said, wrapping his arms around her. "It's very different."

10

WIZARD'S WAND

*T*he next morning, Jacob sprung out of bed, eager to tell Aunt Iz about his success and to show everyone his wand.

"My wand," he said to himself as he picked it up off the bedside table. "Guess I really am a wizard now."

He went to the mirror and posed with the wand, wanting to make sure he looked impressive. He started dueling imaginary opponents, darting across the room, defending a dark-haired, grey-eyed maiden from a thousand foes. He dove and rolled across his bed, impressing himself with his catlike landing.

Jacob cringed as giggles carried through his open window, sure he had been caught dueling with the air. He walked sheepishly over and looked out, but no one was watching him.

Emilia and Claire didn't even look up from their yoga practice on the lawn. Claire had fallen and was enjoying lying in the grass more than performing her exercises. Emilia reached down, trying to convince her to get back up, but Claire yanked Emilia to the ground. The two girls wrestled on their mats, Emilia scolding through her giggles. The pink of Claire's mat screamed against the green of the grass, while Emilia's pale purple blended in with the soothing morning.

Jacob smiled. The colors suited them both perfectly.

He ran from his room and bounded through the house to the yard, where Emilia was still trying to pull Claire off the grass.

Claire finally scrambled to her feet when she saw Jacob running toward them. "Morning," she said. "Would you like to *ohmmmm* with us?" Claire danced around Jacob, flapping her arms. "The psycho bird dance is good for the soul."

"No." Emilia dragged Claire back to her mat. "Yoga is good for focusing your energy so you stop turning all of my things pink, including my cat."

"But don't you think it's an improvement?" At the fiery look on Emilia's face, Claire fled for the house.

"You forgot your mat!" Emilia called after her, but Claire's bright blond hair had already disappeared through the veranda doors. Emilia shook her head and started rolling up the mats. "I really think that girl is worse than I ever was." She looked at Jacob for an answer, but instead of saying anything, Jacob held his wand out to her. She studied the stick for a long moment. "You did it. You healed the tree."

"Yep, and this was its thank you gift." He twirled the wand between his fingers like a baton.

"That's amazing!" Emilia squealed as she flung herself at him. Jacob staggered from the impact before wrapping his arms around her. "You did it so quickly. Now they'll have to let you stay! Does Iz know? She'll be thrilled! Everyone will be." She kissed him on the cheek.

"Careful," Jacob said, even though his stomach purred at her level of enthusiasm. "Don't want to upset anyone."

"What, Dexter?"

"I don't think he'll be too happy about me staying," Jacob said, secretly hoping Dexter had seen the whole thing through the windows.

"Of course he wants you to stay with us." Emilia bent to roll her mat, no longer looking him in the eye. "Don't judge Dexter, Jacob. He really is a great guy."

Jacob tensed. "Mmm-hmm" was the only noise he could make.

Emilia whacked him playfully in the stomach with her mat. "Really, don't. Just try to get to know him. Please."

～

A week later, Jacob could not have been happier with his life at the Mansion House. He had yoga on the lawn with Claire and Emilia in the mornings, three wonderful meals at the huge family table, and lessons with Aunt Iz and Professor Eames. Jacob had been told by everyone that he was doing exceptionally well, and the lessons were increasingly interesting.

Iz spent her time teaching him to channel his power through his wand, and Professor Eames focused on teaching him specific spells. He spent time in the student library reading other books on magic besides the *Big Three*, as Connor liked to call *ATLAS*, *Lingua Veneficium*, and the *Compendium*. And every evening, Emilia would help him make sense of the day's work, tutoring him on particularly difficult spells and concepts. Or sometimes just sitting on the veranda talking, Emilia telling him about the magical world and all its strangeness, and Jacob, in turn, telling her about all the people they had known back in Fairfield.

Jacob sat in Iz's office, enjoying the warmth of the midday sun as it poured through the open window, daydreaming about asking Emilia for help with his spell pronunciation that evening. Not that he needed it, but that was beside the point. He liked being helped, because he had to sit close to Emilia so they could read from the same book.

"Jacob," Iz said, gently calling his attention back to her. "A very important part of learning to effectively use magic is control and concentration. Once you learn to truly focus your mind, you will be able to do amazing things."

Aunt Iz walked over to her shelf and retrieved not a book, as Jacob had expected, but a round fish bowl. She set the bowl on the desk in front of him. Apart from being filled with water, the bowl was empty. There weren't even any marbles at the bottom.

"What I want you to do is create a water vortex. *Vertunda.*"

The water at the top of the bowl began to swirl. Within seconds, the swirling had reached the bottom of the bowl, creating a perfect miniature tornado.

"The principle of creating a vortex is the same at any level, though the energy required does increase with size. The point of this exercise is not only to create the vortex, but also to maintain it for a prolonged period of time."

"How long?" Jacob asked.

"Let's try creating a vortex first. After that, you can work your way up. Your first goal will be five minutes. Now, focus on the water. The incantation is *vertunda*," she said slowly, emphasizing each syllable. "Now speak clearly and picture the water beginning to swirl."

"*Vertunda.*"

~

*I*t was a bright and beautiful Sunday morning. Jacob hadn't set his alarm since yoga didn't happen on Sundays. Aunt Iz believed in taking a day of rest. She and the professor didn't teach, Molly didn't cook, and Samuel let the grounds grow wild. The students all caught up on their work or just took a nice relaxing day.

Jacob crawled lazily out of bed at half past ten, and even though he knew at least Aunt Iz and the professor must have been awake for hours, the house held the staggering stillness of sleep. Jacob didn't even bother changing out of his pajamas before starting down to the kitchen. Only on Sundays were any of them allowed to eat without dressing for the day first.

Voices and rich peals of laughter lured him toward the kitchen before Jacob had even reached the first floor. He recognized that laugh. It was Emilia, and something was making her very happy. He thought of Dexter making her laugh like that, and his stomach tightened.

Jacob reached the kitchen and popped his head through the door, hoping Dexter was still in bed. He didn't even have time to see who was in the kitchen before he was hit square in the face with a fist-full of flour. He sputtered and brushed his eyelids clean.

Emilia leaned on the counter grinning, and Claire rolled on the floor in fits of laughter, her face red from the lack of air.

"Morning to you too, Claire." Jacob shook his head like a wet dog. Flour formed a cloud around him, sending Claire into a fresh fit of hysterics.

Claire shook her head and gasped. "No," she said, struggling to form words. "No." She pointed to Emilia.

Jacob turned to Emilia, but before he could say anything, he was hit in the chest with a fresh clump of flour.

Emilia laughed at Jacob's shocked face, her glee daring him to retaliate.

"Oh, it's on," Jacob said, taking two long strides to the counter.

Emilia had already darted across the kitchen.

Jacob seized the bag of flour and chased Emilia in circles around the room, tossing flour at her like a maniacal flower girl. Jacob leaped over Claire, who lay on the floor threatening to suffocate at any moment. Finally, Jacob caught Emilia with one arm and, pinning her to his side, emptied the rest of the bag on her head as she shrieked. They tumbled to the floor, gasping and laughing.

There was a cough at the kitchen door. The laughter died

instantly as they looked over to find Dexter standing in the doorway.

"Dex," Emilia said breathlessly as she pushed herself off Jacob and stood. "We were going to make pancakes, but, well, I'm not very good at cooking."

"My father is here to see Isadora, and he wanted to say hello to you. I'll tell him you are indisposed." Dexter turned to leave.

"I can get cleaned up." Emilia followed him to the door.

"Don't bother," Dexter said. The door thumped shut behind him.

"*Ablutere*," Emilia muttered, and all of the flour collected itself nicely into the trash can.

"Emi." Jacob put his hand on her shoulder.

"I'm not hungry anymore. I think I'll go shower." She walked out of the room without looking back, but it didn't matter. Jacob could hear the tears in her voice.

"Come on, Claire." Jacob turned back to the kitchen. "I make great pancakes."

As Jacob searched in the pantry for a fresh batch of flour, an unfamiliar voice spoke in the hallway. "Thank you for your time, Isadora. I will contact you again soon. Dexter, shouldn't you be studying? I believe that is, after all, what you are here for."

"Yes, Father."

Dexter's words were followed by the sound of footsteps and the front door closing.

"Ooh, burn," Claire muttered from behind her mixing bowl, which had turned an interesting shade of fuchsia.

11

OUTFOXED

*K*nock, knock, knock.

Jacob rolled over in bed and looked out the window. Moonlight poured in, but there was no Emilia outside.

Knock, knock, knock.

The sound came from behind him. From his bedroom door. Jacob glanced at the clock. 1:30 a.m. Everyone should be in bed by now.

Knock, knock, knock.

It was louder this time, more insistent. Jacob threw off his green comforter and went to the door.

Dexter leaned against the doorframe, looking perfectly well dressed, even in pajamas.

"Dexter?" Jacob asked, still feeling stupid from sleep.

"Sorry to wake you, Jacob, but I'm afraid this couldn't wait." Dexter shouldered past Jacob into the room. Jacob's door closed without him touching it. "First off, I want to apologize. I haven't been as welcoming to you as I should. Emilia means everything to me. She's why I'm here. I want to be with her."

"Right," Jacob said, not really sure how to respond. *I'm here because I want to be with her, too* didn't seem like the best choice.

"You're important to her. She was a wreck when she left you. I even bought her that stupid cat the professor is so in love with to cheer her up. But nothing worked. She always missed you. Now you're here, and she is the happiest I've ever seen her."

Jacob nodded.

"We both care about her. So why should we fight when all we want is what's best for Emilia?" Dexter held out a hand. "Welcome to the Mansion House."

"Thanks."

They shook, and Dexter smiled. "Good, down to business. We have a tradition here at the Mansion House. An initiation of sorts. Emilia doesn't want you to do it. She's too worried about you, thinks you can't do it. But Connor, Claire, and I have all agreed you're ready." Dexter pulled a pink piece of paper from his pajama pocket. "Claire made this up for you. She was going to be the one to tell you about it. But since I wanted to apologize, I thought I should do it instead."

"What is this initiation?" He took the piece of paper from Dexter. It was a typed list of spells.

"Simple. Go into the woods, catch a moon fox, and put it in this." Dexter waved his hand, and a silver cage appeared at Jacob's feet. "Bring it to breakfast tomorrow. The list of spells contains helpful suggestions, in case you need a few ideas."

"Moon fox?" Jacob eyed the cage.

"They really are harmless. I would say you could talk to Emilia about it tomorrow. But tonight is the last night of the full moon, and that's the only time the moon fox comes out."

"Right." Jacob had read about things that only came out during the full moon.

"It's easy. Claire did it when she got here, and she was only seven. If you don't think you're up to it, that's fine." With another wave of Dexter's hand the cage disappeared. "I just thought you might want to show off a bit after all your work."

A war raged in Jacob's mind as he studied Dexter's calm face.

Dexter was trying to be nice, so he should go. Dexter was never nice, so he shouldn't trust him.

"Emilia will be happy you didn't go," Dexter said. "I'll say goodnight."

Dexter walked past Jacob and had his hand on the door before Jacob stopped him.

"So, how do I find this moon fox?"

Dexter smiled.

~

Twenty minutes later, Jacob was trudging through the woods, alone and slightly cold. "*Inluesco.*" He held the orb of light out in front of him, trying to pick his way carefully through the trees. He was off the path now, far beyond his little tree. When the house was no longer in sight, he extinguished the light in his hand and waited in the dark.

He stood still, peering into the night. The cold of the ground numbed his feet. He clenched his fists. If Dexter had sent him out here for nothing…

Then he saw it. A light hovering through the trees. Jacob stalked forward slowly, easing his feet onto the ground, careful to make no noise.

Floating not twelve feet in front of him was a silver fox. The animal glowed the soft white of the full moon and glided through the air like a ghost.

Jacob took another step forward. A twig snapped under his foot.

The fox spun around, growling.

Jacob fumbled for the pink paper, drawing his wand.

"*Inluminaquio,*" he read in the silver glow. Instantly, a light shone down on Jacob. A light so bright he could barely see the fox. But the growling moved toward him.

He shielded his eyes and tried to read the next spell.

"*Procellita.*" The wind whipped around him. Leaves and dirt pelted his face, but through it all gleamed the shining white teeth of the moon fox coming closer.

Jacob cursed and took off, darting through the trees. The bright beam followed like a searchlight emanating from the sky itself. He ran like a fugitive, the wind and branches ripping his clothes. He tried to find a spell on the list that could stop all of this, but before he could read anything, the wind grabbed the pink paper and yanked it away. A growling close to his ear pushed him to run even faster.

His mind raced, fumbling for words. A spell, any spell. "*Crevexo!*" he shouted, aiming his wand behind him. The ground shook beneath his feet, but the growling came closer.

"*Viperelos!*" Something hard and damp coiled around his ankle. He fell face first into the dirt as a tree root snaked around his leg.

"*Mesalvo!*" he screamed, trying to free himself. But nothing happened. In front of him, the fox glowed brightly, only inches away, baring its teeth.

"*Perago canticum!*" a voice called from behind him.

The wind stopped, the light went out, and a red fox fell to the ground with a whimper and ran away.

"Jacob." Emilia ran toward him. "Are you all right?"

"I'm fine." Jacob gasped for air.

"What the hell are you doing out here?" She knelt by his trapped ankle. "*Everto.*"

The root snapped, and Jacob flexed his ankle, trying to get blood back into his foot. "You don't know?"

"I was asleep until that crazy light woke me up. Why were you trying to capture moonlight?" She pulled Jacob to his feet.

"To catch a moon fox," a voice answered from behind them. Dexter walked out through the trees, smiling.

Emilia cast a death glare at Dexter, and for the first time, Jacob was glad she wasn't looking at him.

"Moon fox, Dex? There is no such thing as a moon fox," she snarled.

"I know that. It was just a silly prank. We were bonding, right?" Dexter's smile faltered.

"Bonding in the middle of the night? Were you watching the whole time? Did you see the spell he was trying to use? And you." She rounded on Jacob, who suddenly missed the growling fox. "Why would you come out here looking for a moon fox? Were you going to try and find a leprechaun, too? I've heard Aunt Iz wants to keep them in the yard now. And don't forget the dragon in the garage. Claire really loves her new pet! And where on earth did you get those spells? Do you have any idea how dangerous a maelstrom spell can be?"

"I got them off the paper—" Jacob glanced at Dexter, whose face paled in the moonlight. Claire had nothing to do with that paper.

"Em," Dexter murmured.

"Just go," Emilia said. "I'll talk to you tomorrow."

Jacob waited for Dexter to argue, but he turned and walked away.

Emilia stayed silent until Dexter disappeared from view. "Are you sure you're not hurt?"

"I'm fine," Jacob said. "I'll know better than to listen to him again."

Emilia started walking down the path, leaving space for Jacob to walk beside her. "The thing is, after Fairfield, I sort of fell apart. He was there for me. He might not be the easiest to deal with all the time, but he loves me, Jacob." She shook her head. Her hair floated down and covered her face.

Jacob wanted to push the hair away. To tell her he loved her. That he would be there for her always.

She stopped and looked into Jacob's eyes. "And I love him. Even if he is a jerk sometimes. Even if I may have to murder him tomorrow. I'm sorry about all of this. I'll make sure he stops. He won't bother you again."

Pain cracked in Jacob's chest as though his heart had been ripped out. She loved him. She had just said it. Emilia loved Dexter.

"Emilia?" a voice whispered from the back door.

"Great," Emilia murmured.

They jogged up to the veranda doors where Claire waited in her pink pajamas.

"What are you doing out here?" Claire asked, smirking as she glanced from Emilia to Jacob. "I woke up, and there was a weird light, so I went to your room and you were gone."

"Did you wake anyone else up?" Emilia asked.

"No," Claire answered defensively. "I came to see what the fun was."

"Don't worry about it, Claire," Jacob said as he slipped inside. "I was just out hunting."

12

THE TABOO MAGIC

*J*acob tried to avoid the library the next day. Dexter was in there, and he didn't want to deal with him. Jacob kept picturing himself throwing things at Dexter's head, and the temptation was becoming almost too strong to resist. But he needed to get some work done, and Emilia was off in the woods somewhere anyway.

So Jacob entered the library, sat at his desk, and pulled out his copy of *Lingua Venificium*, trying to concentrate on his book instead of all the things he wanted to scream at Dexter. How could Emilia love someone like that? He opened the book and began to read.

Shielding Spells

A Personal Shield Spell is most effective when being used to guard the spellcaster only. A P.S.S. may also be used to cover others, but all persons to be covered by the shield must maintain physical contact with the spellcaster at all times. The P.S.S. incantation is Primurgo.

Group Shield Spells are spells that are meant to shield a place rather than a specific person. While G.S.S. are possible, a group or casting circle is needed to maintain a strong shield. Many groups choose to create their own shielding spells to prevent their shield from being easily penetrated by attackers. The most common incantation for a G.S.S. is Primionis.

Jacob shoved the book away. Shield spells weren't holding his attention.

Dexter closed his book and placed it into his desk drawer. The lock clicked loudly. Dexter smiled at Jacob and sauntered out of the room, whistling.

Jacob wanted to chase Dexter down the hall and tackle him. Or at least throw something hard and heavy at the back of his head. Like a desk. Or a fist.

The front door slammed. He looked at Dexter's desk. What had he been so obnoxiously snooty about? It was just a book, and Jacob was allowed to read all the books in the house.

He got up quietly and took his *Lingua Veneficium* over to Dexter's desk. He glanced back through the open door before flipping to the page for unlocking. *"Compuere."* The lock clicked. Jacob pulled out a little brown book entitled *The Taboo Magic*. It seemed like an odd book for Dexter to be treating so possessively. *"Proprioris,"* Jacob said, and the book flipped itself to the last page it had opened to. He turned back a few pages to find the beginning of the section.

Tethering

The magical binding of two people. Historically, tethering was an integral part of a wizarding wedding. After a tethering ceremony, the coniunx, *or tethered couple, would gain the ability to sense one another and would develop a greatly increased emotional attachment.*

In today's wizarding society, tethering is rarely included in wedding ceremonies. It is generally considered archaic and makes divorce much more difficult, as a tethering can only be severed by the death of one of the coniunx. *The demise of half of the pair is incredibly painful for the remaining party and often results in their subsequent death.*

Jacob tossed the book back into the drawer as though it were poisonous and continued contact would contaminate him. He locked the drawer and hurried back to his desk. No wonder

Dexter hadn't wanted him to see the book. If Dexter thought Emilia would ever tether herself to someone like him, to anyone—

Jacob's water glass exploded. As he bent to pick up the pieces, all he could picture was Dexter's head exploding instead.

13

FULGURATUS

"*Aperestra ab externum. Arcanestra ab externum.*" The shutters in Jacob's room swung open and closed as he paced and nervously repeated the spells to himself. He had been at the Mansion House for a month now, and the professor had decided it was time for his first formal test. Not that the grades could be reported to anyone, but Jacob still wanted to do well.

Emilia had stayed up late into the night helping him study. She had even snuck back to her room by walking on the roof shingles so Dexter wouldn't know how late she'd stayed.

Jacob checked the clock. 8:56 a.m. Time to head down for his lesson.

"*Elevare,*" Jacob muttered under his breath, levitating the pencil in his hand as he walked down the stairs.

He arrived at the professor's office, but the door was shut. Jacob raised his hand to knock before realizing there were voices on the other side of the door. One voice belonged to Professor Eames, but there was another deep, rumbling voice Jacob didn't recognize.

"Are you quite sure Willow was taken?" Professor Eames asked. "I know it may be difficult for you to consider, but is there a possibility she left on her own? She is nearly an adult, after all."

The other voice answered, but Jacob couldn't make out the words.

"If MAGI is looking for her," the professor said, "I'm sure she will soon be found. I'll contact Larkin and make sure she takes a look at Willow's file. And Proteus, my friend, I promise to do what"—there was a pause—"poking about I can."

The low voice rumbled again.

"Yes, he's probably outside right now. It's nearly time for his lesson. Jacob," the professor called, "please come in."

Jacob entered the study and looked around for the owner of the low voice, but the professor was alone.

"Good morning, Jacob," the professor greeted him, smiling. "I would like you to meet my friend, Proteus." He indicated a mirror on his desk.

Jacob crossed around the desk to look into the mirror. Staring back at him was the most strangely fascinating man Jacob had ever seen.

His eyes held a fierce and wild look that was both intimidating and worthy of hero worship. Grey streaked his long, curly black hair, which flowed past his bare, well muscled shoulders. His chiseled face was tan and weathered, and his eyes an unnaturally bright shade of blue.

The man in the mirror surveyed Jacob. "Jacob, it is very nice to meet you. I hope someday soon we shall meet in person." He nodded to the professor, and with that the mirror became a reflection of the room.

"How did you do that?" Jacob asked, examining the seemingly normal mirror.

"That was skrying. Magical people learned long ago how to communicate with each other through mirrors." The professor's eyes twinkled. "You don't think humans came up with Skype on their own, do you?"

Jacob shook his head in amazement. "So that other wizard just called your mirror?"

"Well, normal skrying works rather like a telephone. One party will attempt to contact another. The second party has the ability to accept or decline the communication. There is a form of skrying that can be done without the acceptance of the second party, but it is, shall we say, frowned upon." The professor moved the mirror onto the shelf and started rearranging his desk to prepare for the morning lesson. "And incidentally, Proteus isn't a wizard. He's a centaur."

Jacob tried to picture the man he had just seen in the mirror. "He looked so…human."

"Centaurs generally do from the waist up," the professor said as he picked up his wand. "Now, let us begin your examination with a few basics. Please demonstrate three different ways to form a magical light in this room."

～

*I*t took more than three hours for Jacob to finish the professor's test. He lit the room, made water froth, changed the color of the professor's clothing, and created a shield spell strong enough to block the pennies the professor tossed at him. He finished the test hungry and tired, but proud of himself.

"Well done, Jacob." Professor Eames clapped as Jacob levitated a pencil from the desk into his hand. "Well done, indeed! I must say I am very impressed. Isadora will be pleased. Why don't we go and brag about your progress over lunch, and then we can spend the afternoon working outside. I have quite the treat planned for you."

Everyone had already started eating when they took their seats at the large dining room table.

"Well, everyone," the professor said jovially, helping himself to a large portion of pasta salad, "Jacob has just done very well on his first test."

"That is wonderful, Jacob," Iz said.

Emilia smiled at Jacob from across the table, while Connor, who sat next to him, reached over and patted him on the back.

"I knew you weren't going to be completely useless," Connor said with a grin.

The only people who didn't seem happy about Jacob's success were Dexter, which was to be expected, and Claire, who was uncharacteristically silent and dressed in black. Jacob had never before seen Claire without some shade of pink in her clothing.

Emilia followed Jacob's gaze. "Don't mind her." She fixed Claire with a disapproving stare. "She's pouting."

"I am not pouting," Claire replied, her voice clipped and her nose in the air. "I am in mourning."

"Claire lost her computer privileges for the next month," Iz said, passing the cranberry juice. "Her computer is locked in my office, and she is not to borrow anyone else's."

"But I need my laptop," Claire groaned. "I'm not whole without it." She tipped her head all the way back and stared at the ceiling, crossing her arms tightly.

"Then you should stop trying to hack into other people's computer files and learn to mind your own business." Dexter shook his fork at Claire.

Claire pounded both fists on the table. "I didn't try to hack into anything. I succeeded. And maybe I was doing something really nice and important."

Dexter laughed. "Of course you were. What were you trying to do, find a way to buy next month's clothes today? That is very important."

Tears glistened in the corners of Claire's eyes. "What would you know about doing something nice?"

"Children," Iz said, a quiet warning in her voice.

"I didn't start it. Wonder Woman over there did." Claire

crossed her arms in front of her face and sang the Wonder Woman theme song.

Jacob grinned, and Emilia dipped her head toward her plate to hide her smile. Dexter fumed in his seat, twisting the cuffs on his wrists. Somehow his anger made the Wonder Woman cracks twice as funny.

"I think I've finished eating now." Dexter stood. "Thank you for lunch, Molly." He strode quickly from the room.

Everyone else finished eating in silence.

"We should go outside for our afternoon lesson now, Jacob." The professor rubbed his hands together as Molly cleared away the plates. "I do think you will enjoy it."

They went outside onto the sun kissed lawn.

Dexter lay in the grass next to, what appeared to be, a giant, floating dartboard.

"Ah, Dexter," Professor Eames said as Dexter sat up lazily, "thank you for joining us." He went over to the dartboard and rapped on it. "Good, feels nice and sturdy." He turned to Jacob with a smile. "Today we are going to work on Lightning Darts, or Shards as some call them. It is a very simple offensive device, and this"—he patted the dartboard—"will help with your aim. No talisman, for now. We don't want the darts to get too powerful."

Dexter pulled off his cuffs and laid them carefully on the grass next to his phone. He grinned at Jacob before standing up and facing the dartboard. *"Fulguratus."* A small, silver lightning bolt appeared in his hand. It crackled and sparked like real lightning, but it didn't burn Dexter as he rolled it through his fingers. Then, in one fluid motion, he threw the lightning at the board. It struck the very center, leaving a tiny singe mark. "Bull's eye."

"Very good, Dexter." The professor beamed. "I thought it might be nice for you to have someone to practice with, Jacob, and Dexter is fond of this game."

"Great." Jacob tried to sound enthusiastic.

The professor nodded fervently. "Now, the spell to create the bolt is *fulguratus*. And to formulate the energy, I want you to picture a lightning bolt in your hand. You must picture the shape of the bolt very clearly, then fill it in with your energy. Go on, have a try."

Jacob flexed his right hand and tried to picture a lightning bolt. He imagined the zigzag edges and the bright light it would emanate. *"Fulguratus."* For a moment, the center of his hand shone with a white light. Jacob jumped, so shocked by his success his concentration faltered, and the light faded.

"Very good," the professor said.

Dexter, however, looked unimpressed.

"Try again, try again," the professor said.

Trying again would have been a lot easier without Dexter standing there judging him. Jacob shook his hand and tried to focus. He pictured the lightning bolt crackling with energy in his palm. *"Fulguratus."*

This time the bolt stayed, and as he watched, it turned into a real, tangible object that was both cool and smooth in his hand. Jacob ran his thumb along its edge, the energy of the shard humming through his skin.

The professor clapped and cheered. "Now throw it at the board!"

Jacob took careful aim and threw the sparking, shimmering bolt at the target, missing the center by inches.

"Haha! Wonderful." Professor Eames laughed. "It looks like you might have some competition, Dexter."

Dexter glowered. He placed his hand in the air, palm up, and a bolt appeared without incantation. "I always enjoy competition."

They spent the next hour practicing with the dartboard. Jacob improved rapidly. Gym class had finally come in handy. All those years of dodgeball had taught him something about hand-eye coordination.

"Excellent!" the professor exclaimed as Jacob hit his first

perfect bull's eye. "Now all you need is to work on formulating the bolt more quickly."

"Thank you, Professor," Jacob said, wishing the library window faced the garden. Then Emilia would have been able to watch his success.

"Joseph," Molly called from the veranda. It took Jacob a moment to realize she meant Professor Eames. "Joseph, I would like to speak to you inside, please." Molly hurried toward them. She was pale, and her forehead was lined with creases.

"Is everyone all right?" Jacob asked. With so much magic in the house, it was always possible for someone to get struck by a badly aimed spell.

"Yes, yes everyone is fine, boys. Professor, now please." Molly took Professor Eames by the arm and led him back to the house.

Jacob moved to follow them inside, but Dexter stepped in front of him, blocking his path.

"Done already?" Dexter asked. "We could keep playing. We could even spar."

"Spar?" Jacob asked, his hackles rising at the tone in Dexter's voice.

"The board is only for target practice, and you seem to be doing well enough with that. So we might as well spar."

"I don't think Professor Eames would like that." Jacob pushed past him toward the house.

"That was the plan for today anyway. He had me come out here so we could spar. Unless you feel uncomfortable without the babysitter." Dexter sneered.

Heat rose in his chest as he turned to face Dexter. "Fine. We'll spar. What do we do?"

"Stay." Dexter pointed to Jacob as though he were a badly behaved dog before striding twenty feet away. Then, without any warning, he turned back to Jacob and shot a lightning bolt straight into his stomach.

Jacob fell to the ground with a grunt as if he'd been kicked by an angry centaur. All of the air had been knocked out of his lungs.

Dexter paced in front of the target. "Now it's your turn." Dexter watched as Jacob struggled to his feet. "Really, you should go immediately after me, but that's all right. I don't mind waiting."

Jacob formed a shard in his hand. He focused and threw it straight at Dexter, but Dexter threw a bolt of his own, which knocked Jacob's to the ground, singeing a patch of grass.

Dexter laughed. "Blocking is fundamental. I'm sure you'll pick it up." He threw a bolt into Jacob's knee, which buckled and sent him back to the ground. "Eventually," Dexter added with a grin.

Jacob didn't bother standing up before forming a bolt of his own, which grazed Dexter's shoulder but didn't stop his laughing.

"Emilia will be proud." Dexter brushed the embers off his shoulder.

"You must really hate that I turned out to be a wizard after all," Jacob said as he heaved himself up off the ground. "Bet you thought I would never show up."

"On the contrary," Dexter said, casually throwing a lightning shard from hand to hand, "if she had never seen you again, Emilia would have spent the rest of her life hating herself for leaving you. Now you're here, and the guilt is gone. There are no more *what ifs*. Emilia can truly be mine."

Jacob didn't reply, but Dexter correctly interpreted his silence.

"Oh, I know you'll fight for her." Dexter laughed as he sent another lightning shard into Jacob's stomach. "But I'll win."

"Dexter!" a voice shouted from the patio. Connor ran toward them. "What the hell?" He stopped next to Jacob, who was doubled over from the last blow. "You all right?"

"Fine," Jacob grunted. "Dexter was just teaching me about sparring."

"Well, if Aunt Iz finds out about this, Dexter will be in it so deep he won't be sparring for a long time." Connor glared at Dexter.

"It was all in good fun," Dexter said with an easy smile. "Not my fault he doesn't know how to play. And you had best watch your mouth. *Lavlui*." Soap bubbles appeared in Dexter's hand, and he threw them at Connor before striding to the house, whistling.

"Are you sure you're all right?" Connor asked as soon as Dexter was out of earshot. "Emilia will fry him for this. I don't know what his problem is. He's always been a—" He used a word that made Jacob laugh.

"Don't let Molly hear you saying that," Jacob warned.

Connor shrugged. "But Dexter's never been like this."

"Don't tell Emilia," Jacob said. "I can manage Dexter myself."

"Okay, but why don't you spar with me for a while? I won't go easy on you, but at least I'm not a psycho."

14

WHAT TOMORROW MAY BRING

*T*hat night, after most of the house was asleep, Jacob lay awake in his room, searching the *Compendium* for information on famous duels. He was too worked up from the day to sleep, and pain still shot through his knee from Dexter's well-aimed blow. The knee wasn't too swollen, just stiff and sore. Jacob wanted to ice it, but getting ice might mean running into Molly, and he was sure she would want to know exactly what he had done.

Jacob sighed and lay back on his pillow. A book dug into his spine. He pulled *Lingua Veneficium* out from under himself and stared at the spell book for a moment. Surely there must be an ice-making spell in it somewhere. The professor had warned him not to try new spells alone, and the stupid fox incident had gone badly. But if he did one, tiny spell, no one would ever need to know. He glanced around the room, half expecting Professor Eames to jump out of a shadow wagging one of his wrinkly fingers.

He flipped through the book until he came across an entry: *To Freeze*—Strigo motus. *Aim the talisman at the desired target and voice spell.*

That was easier than any of the other spells Jacob had tried with Professor Eames.

Jacob read the words out loud a few times to make sure he had the pronunciation right, then picked up his wand and aimed at his hurt knee. *"Strigo motus."* His knee shimmered for a moment. Jacob sighed as the pain vanished.

He went to stand up to put his books away, but when he put his legs over the side of the bed, his right leg stayed straight as a board. Jacob tried to bend it, but it wouldn't move. He touched his knee but couldn't feel anything. His knee didn't feel cold. It didn't feel at all. Jacob cursed.

He tried again to bend his knee, but it had frozen in place. He flipped *Lingua Veneficium* back to the Freeze spell. There was no counter spell written next to it. Or cross reference. Or alternate translation.

Jacob cursed again. He didn't want to risk piling another spell on top of this one, and he might need to be able to bend his knee again at some point in his life. He needed help.

There was no way he could go to Iz. She would want to know why he was hurt. The professor would be angry Jacob had tried the spell. Molly would worry. He would rather cut his leg off than ask Dexter for help. He was sure Emilia could fix it, but she would ask too many questions. And he didn't want to tell her about what had happened with the sparring. Connor and Claire he didn't trust with the safety of his leg.

The only one left was Samuel. Samuel didn't seem like the type who would ask too many questions.

Jacob pushed himself off the bed and wobbled out of the room to find Samuel, dragging his useless leg behind him. He managed all right until he got to the stairs and almost fell a few times trying to move quietly in the dark. But eventually, he made it to the ground floor by sitting on his butt and scooting along one stair at a time, pausing every few seconds to check that no one was coming. The thought of being found like that was too humiliating to contemplate.

Samuel lived right off the kitchen in a small stable that used to house animals. It had been renovated so he could have a door that opened to the gardens instead of a hallway.

When Jacob arrived at the stable, he found Samuel sitting outside in a rocking chair, gazing at the stars. Samuel didn't seem to notice Jacob's ungainly approach.

"Um, Samuel?" Jacob said as he reached the rocking chair. "Do you have a minute?"

Samuel blinked and turned toward Jacob. "Sure. What do you need?"

How could he ask for help without mentioning how he had gotten hurt? Was there another logical explanation for freezing his own leg? "Well, it's nothing really. I...ah, well, I didn't know who else to go to, and I really, really don't want anyone else to know."

Samuel leaned forward, frowning. "Right."

"So, I was hoping maybe you could help me but not tell anyone," Jacob said. "Especially not Aunt Iz or Emilia."

"All right. I'll do what I can to help, and I won't tell. Unless it's something Isadora really needs to know."

Jacob stood silent for a moment. Was this the sort of thing Aunt Iz would *really* need to know? But Jacob couldn't see another solution to his problem. "I froze my knee," he mumbled. Jacob braced himself for Samuel to yell at him. But instead, Samuel laughed.

"Is that all?" He shook his head and pinched the bridge of his nose. "I have to admit, from the way you were talking. Whew!"

"What did you think I meant?" Jacob asked.

"Nothing, it's just, with the way kids are these days..." Samuel raised his eyebrows. "Knees, I can fix." He pulled up another chair. "Sit, let me see."

Jacob sat with his right leg sticking straight out in front of him and pulled up his pant leg.

Samuel examined Jacob's knee. "What spell did you use?"

"*Strigo motus.*"

"Right. Easy fix." Standing, Samuel grabbed his staff, placed one end on the ground, and said, "*Cantus relovare.*"

Painful sensation flooded back into Jacob's knee. A thousand hot needles pricked his leg, all searching for the spot that would hurt him the worst. Jacob breathed in through his teeth.

"It'll hurt for a bit, but there'll be no lasting damage. You should sit still till the pain stops. It'll be a few minutes." Samuel sat back down.

"Thanks," Jacob said through gritted teeth.

"Mind telling me why you decided to try a spell on yourself?"

"I thought it would be like icing it," Jacob answered. "My knee was bothering me."

"From your little bout with Dexter?"

"How did you know?" Jacob asked.

"Connor told me. And don't be angry with him for doing it. He wanted to know if he should tell Isadora or the professor about it. Connor was worried about you. He's a good kid."

"What did you tell him?" Jacob asked.

"That what's between you and Dexter should stay that way. Connor was right to stop Dexter this morning. But I have known Dexter Wayland for some time, and whatever you did to make him angry, it's best you two sort it out on your own." Samuel looked at Jacob. "Unless, of course, you want help?"

"No." Jacob shook his head. "I want to deal with him on my own."

"That's what I thought. Sometimes we have to fight for what we want. And if you want something enough, the fight will be worth it."

"Yeah," Jacob said. Did Samuel know more than he let on about why he and Dexter were really fighting? It sounded like

Samuel wanted Jacob to win. He knew he had always liked Samuel for a reason.

They sat in silence for a few minutes.

"Why are you still awake?" Jacob asked. "If you don't mind my asking," he added quickly.

"We all have fights ahead of us. Some are coming sooner than you'd think. And sometimes you need to decide what you're willing to give to win before you go into a fight."

"You're talking about the Dragons, aren't you?" Jacob asked, already sure of the answer.

Samuel nodded.

"Is it getting that bad?"

"Isadora and Professor Eames don't want to worry all of you. But yes, it is getting that bad. And the word is, tomorrow it'll get worse."

"If the rebels are so set on humans finding out about wizards, why don't they just tell them?" Jacob massaged the blood back into his knee.

Samuel didn't answer right away. He stared up at the stars, as though waiting for them to answer for him.

"It's easy, really. Let's say a month ago I met you on the street and told you I was a wizard," Samuel said. "You would have thought I was crazy. Suppose I tried to prove it by showing you my powers. You would have said it was an optical illusion or some new technology. So instead I go to a news station or a government official and make a public announcement. The government would assume I was seeking publicity, or I was insane and possibly dangerous, in which case I would be imprisoned and have to go through the trouble of escaping and going on some wanted list."

Samuel shook his head, tracing shapes in the dirt with his staff. Jacob wished he knew what or who crept through Samuel's thoughts. A breeze flowed from the base of Samuel's staff, scattering the dust of the drawings away.

"The only way to convince the general population of the existence of magic is by a show of force involving so many wizards the truth would become undeniable," Samuel said. "But a demonstration of that size is a very hard thing to organize without the Council or MAGI noticing. Whatever the rebels are planning must be big. The only way to gain from a public display like that is to scare humans into submission.

"We can only assume it will be grisly enough to scare the general population into allowing Magickind some form of power. People won't automatically assume wizards are behind the attack. They're more likely to jump to militarized terrorists of the human variety, or, in some places, the work of the devil. But they won't be able to deny something is happening. That a new kind of power is rising. Terrifying thought, isn't it?"

"What sort of thing would the Dragons do to scare people?" Jacob asked.

"Don't know. But the Dragons have let the word spread they're planning something big. We don't know what, but they want us to be watching when it happens. So we wait for what tomorrow may bring."

"Then what?"

"The fight begins. Never be afraid to fight for what you believe in, Jacob. Or for what you love." Samuel stood up. "Your leg should be better by now. Best to get some sleep."

"Goodnight," Jacob said as Samuel closed his door.

～

*J*acob lay in bed, staring at the ceiling, thinking of Emilia. How many times she had climbed through his window. How many days it had been just the two of them at school. And it had never mattered how bad things were as long as he had her. Emilia smiling. Emilia laughing.

He was in love with her.

The thought of Dexter kissing her, protecting her, made a snake curl in his stomach. He had always been in love with Emilia, and now he was going to do something about it. He would fight for her with everything he had.

And the Dragons? He pictured the vague threat the Grays all feared. It didn't feel like his fight. A few people he had never met were missing. Some settlements he had never even heard of were being threatened. The Council was only a faraway authority to him.

But Emilia.

He took a breath, and for a moment he could smell her scent as though she were lying next to him. If it was her fight, then it would have to be his, too. There was nothing he wouldn't give to protect her. He didn't know what was coming, but Samuel was right. All he could do was wait for what tomorrow may bring.

As Jacob slid into sleep, visions of fire and floods pulled him into darkness.

15

THE BREAKING POINT

"Claire, put the computer away. You know you're still grounded," Emilia said, her voice hinting at a warning. She didn't need to look over her shoulder to know whose computer keys were clacking away behind her. Emilia went back to her reading.

The ability to align oneself with the cardinal directions is a fundamental skill that is often overlooked.

Click, click, click.

"Put the computer away, Claire. You're going to get in trouble again if Aunt Iz catches you."

"I can't." Claire's voice was strange, dull.

Emilia turned.

Tears streamed down Claire's face. Her lips trembled.

"What's wrong?" Emilia asked.

Claire stood and tore from the room.

"Claire!" Emilia followed her, ready to run outside and take care of whatever horrible drama had gripped her today. But Claire stood in the living room, eyes fixed on the big TV, the remote hanging forgotten in her hand.

Water raced everywhere. People screamed as a fire blazed in the distance.

"Requests for aid are being sent out all over the country, but the explosion at the Neversink Dam was catastrophic. There are simply not enough first responders. Homes and businesses have already flooded, and the waters continue to rise. Tragically, the force of the water was so intense that those caught unaware had very little chance for survival.

"Emergency crews are currently focusing on evacuating the outlying areas to prevent further casualties. The number of missing is still unknown, and confirmed deaths are already in the hundreds. Authorities have said that, at this point, it is impossible to determine what the death toll may ultimately be."

The reporter continued with information about evacuation sites and numbers to call for help locating loved ones. A government official warned civilians to stay away. The roads near the dam were too hazardous to risk travel. There was nothing to do but let the emergency crews try to evacuate as many people as possible. At least two towns would be lost before the flood could be stopped.

An arm wrapped around Emilia's waist.

"What happened, Dex?" she asked.

"It was the Dragons," Samuel answered from the hall before Dexter could respond. "I just got a call from Larkin. I need to head out."

"But how do they know?" Connor asked, not looking away from the horrors on the screen.

"They track everything." Tears streamed down Claire's face. "Something like this...Spellnet would see it."

Samuel left without another word.

Dexter threaded his fingers through Emilia's and led her to the couch. She buried herself in his warmth, wanting to wake up in her bed. Safe, without flooding, without death.

"What's wrong?" Jacob asked, and Emilia turned toward his voice. He stood in the hall, pink-faced and smiling.

"Jacob." She scrambled over the back of the couch and threw her arms around him. He was warm from the sun. She breathed in his scent of grass and life.

"There's been an attack," Dexter said. He held his hand out to Emilia, drawing her back to the reality of attacks and death. "The Dragons destroyed a dam."

"How do you know it was the Dragons?" Jacob asked.

The television now showed live footage from a helicopter flying over the water as it raced into another panic-swept town. Emilia couldn't tear her gaze from the devastation on the screen. Her stomach rolled at the idea that this massacre had been manufactured.

Dexter's arm closed around her again, and she let him lead her back to the couch. But she held onto Jacob's hand, pulling him along with her. She couldn't let go of him. It was too hard to find air. Wizards had done this. Wizards had killed all those people.

"Maybe it was an accident. I blew up a school," Jacob said.

"This was too deliberate," Dexter said. "Too perfect. The way the dam cracked, and how many towns the water is going to reach. The Dragons are making a statement to Magickind. They can attack. They can kill en masse, and the humans won't even know how it happened. They killed those people on purpose." Dexter stroked Emilia's hair, tucking it behind her ear. "The game just changed, Em. There's no point in hiding from it."

They waited for hours, grouped in the living room, staring at the television in numb horror. Watching helplessly as limp children were carried by hysterical mothers. Students stood on the roof of their school, calling desperately for help. Soaked emergency workers fought to pull just one more survivor from the racing waters. A man in a suit stood on a podium to make the announcement: the dam's collapse had been deliberate. This was an attack. The entire country had been placed on high alert.

Molly kept pacing to and from the kitchen with tears in her

eyes. Iz and Professor Eames had locked themselves in Iz's study. Finally, Iz came out looking, for the first time in Emilia's memory, old. The living room group moved to the door to meet her.

"The Council has called an emergency meeting," Aunt Iz said.

Everyone nodded. This was expected under the circumstances.

"Jacob," Aunt Iz said, "they have requested your presence."

"What?" Jacob asked.

Professor Eames stepped forward and looked Jacob in the eye. "In light of this morning's events, the Council now feels an immediate inquiry into the incident at Fairfield High School is required." The professor addressed the rest of the family. "Jacob is to present himself to the Council at noon tomorrow. He will be tried by the Council for the destruction of Fairfield High School and questioned about the events at the Neversink Dam."

"He had nothing to do with this." Emilia stepped in front of Jacob, protecting him from an unseen danger. "They can't use him as a scapegoat. He's been here with us."

"And we will convince them of that." The professor held up a hand to halt Emilia's protests. "He has no choice but to attend the meeting. Now, go and pack your bag, Jacob. You will be leaving for the airport as soon as possible." The professor turned to Dexter. "Your father is going to the Council meeting, of course, and he would like you to stay with your family in New York. He has sent a helicopter for you, which should be arriving shortly."

"I'm going to New York, too." Emilia slipped her hand into Jacob's. "He's not going without me."

"Of course," Aunt Iz said. "I expected as much."

"I'll make arrangements for you two with Molly," the professor said, patting Claire and Connor on the shoulders before leaving for the kitchen.

"I'll pack for you." Claire's voice shook. "You wouldn't do it right anyway." As Claire ran up the stairs, Emilia thought she heard a stifled sob.

"I'll be right back," Emilia said before racing to her room to throw things into a suitcase.

Dexter followed without a word.

Emilia closed her eyes and tried to breathe. The panic in her chest didn't subside.

She pulled her suitcase from under the bed and tried to pack calmly, but her hands refused to stop shaking. Her dresser drawers opened before she could reach them. All her clothes were a mess. Shirts or sweaters? And pants, she needed pants. One sweater seemed determined not to fold. Emilia threw it onto the bed with a frustrated shriek.

Arms slipped around her waist. Emilia sank into the warmth of the body behind her. "Dex, I…" She couldn't finish explaining why she needed to go to New York.

Dexter turned her around, comforting her with a kiss. He stepped around her and folded the offending sweater.

"Thanks," Emilia said as he slid the sweater into her suitcase.

"Emilia," Dexter said, zipping her bag, "I just spoke to my father. The helicopter has an open seat. Come with me."

"Dex."

"The ride will be shorter, and you can meet Iz at the house in New York." Dexter lifted Emilia's bag.

She placed her hand on top, pressing the case to the bed. "I have to stay with Jacob. Help brief him for the meeting."

"I'm sure Iz can do that."

"But I want to help," Emilia said, hating the look of disappointment in his eyes. "I'm sorry, Dex." She kissed him lightly. "I'll call you when we land."

Emilia took her suitcase from Dexter and headed downstairs. When she got to the living room, everyone had already gathered. Aunt Iz had booked the tickets, and Professor Eames was bringing around the Cadillac since Samuel had already left with the BMW. Molly had prepared bags of traveling snacks, and Claire had packed Jacob's suitcase, which was larger than Emilia's.

The family slowly trickled outside, like mourners congregating for a funeral. Connor carried the suitcases to the car before slipping back into the house. Emilia wanted to say goodbye to Dexter, but he was already waiting in the clearing for his father's helicopter.

"Emilia," Aunt Iz said from the driver's seat.

Emilia slipped into the back of the car. Molly clung to Jacob for a moment before bustling back to the kitchen. Jacob climbed in next to Emilia. Claire waved as Professor Eames led her inside.

As Aunt Iz drove away from the Mansion House, Jacob looked back. Emilia prayed he would be with them when they returned.

1 6

DRAGON'S FLIGHT

*T*hey arrived just in time to check in and get through security. Even through his fear, Jacob found the airport fascinating. What would it look like from high above in the plane? Tiny ants piling into a big bug that could fly? The whole process seemed absurd.

"Shoes," Emilia said as they loaded their belongings onto the conveyor belt that fed the x-ray machine.

"Huh?" Jacob asked, still focused on a man who had been pulled aside after the metal detector declared him a threat.

"You have to put your shoes through the x-ray." Emilia rolled her eyes and leaned in to whisper. "And these people would think traveling by magic was crazy."

"So you could really fly on a broom or a carpet?" Jacob asked in a hushed tone.

"Sure." Emilia prepared her bag for the x-ray machine.

"So why are we here?" Jacob asked.

"The wind chill is awful, there's a huge risk of being sighted, and you can't pack very many shoes," Emilia whispered back. "Some people choose brooms, but I'll fly in a climate-controlled plane any day."

"Claire would hate brooms. No shoes? How ever would she survive the lack of outfit coordination?" Jacob tried to laugh but stopped immediately. The laugh sounded cold and wrong somehow. He watched people being shuttled through the body scanners as he waited for his backpack and shoes.

What would it be like to fly on a broom? He could fly wherever he wanted. No roads or tickets to worry about. He could fly away from the Council. He wouldn't have to stand trial. He could take Emilia and just go. Find someplace sunny and warm neither of them had ever been.

Aunt Iz led them quickly through the airport. They arrived at their gate just as first class passengers were being called to board.

As soon as they were seated, Aunt Iz handed Jacob a golden folder embossed with the lettering *C.O.E.: Persons, Procedures, and Potential Problems.* "This has everything you need to know, and don't worry too much about the details. The most important thing is to be respectful."

Jacob opened the file and began reading. The first few sheets were filled with pictures of Council members and brief biographies outlining personal accomplishments, family histories, and notable attributes of the land they controlled. Next to each Council member was a picture of their Clan crest. Jacob touched the tree of life symbol by Aunt Iz's picture before moving on to the others. He counted thirteen Council members in all.

"Do they represent all the territories in America?" Jacob whispered to Emilia.

"Some of the territories are much larger than others," Emilia said. "It depends on what the population of the area was when the Council was formed. The territories in the east are much smaller in terms of land than the ones in the west."

Jacob nodded. The plane raced down the runway, gaining speed. The front wheels lifted off the ground, pushing Jacob back against his seat. He didn't like the feeling it gave him in his stomach. It felt too much like the dread that had already taken up residence there.

He read for a few minutes, moving on to the *Procedures* section. "What does *Hosting Authority* mean?"

"There used to be a problem with the different Clan heads trying to take more power than was rightfully theirs," Emilia said. "One of the problems was who should be in charge of Council meetings, and who should get to host the meetings. Some people would try to host meetings in the most ridiculous places, hoping some Council members wouldn't be able to find the meeting to vote. The best solution was to always have the meetings in an easy-to-reach place, so they chose New York City."

"But isn't that a bit conspicuous? I mean, wizards gathering with so many humans around?"

Emilia shook her head. "New York is packed with so many kinds of people, no one ever notices anything. The next problem was finding a place. One Elder bought a home in Manhattan and said all the meetings could be held at his house, but no one would agree since his Clan would always have home field advantage.

"So all thirteen Elders now have New York houses, and the meetings rotate between them. Helps to ensure none of the neighbors notice a bunch of wizards meeting. And whoever's house the meeting is in gets to conduct the meeting, and the scribe is also provided from the ranks of that Clan, which helps distribute power more evenly. No one but the thirteen Clan Elders and the scribe are allowed into meetings, not unless they're part of a trial."

Jacob went back to his folder. Iz snored quietly in the seat next to him while Emilia read over his shoulder.

The rules for the trial seemed simple enough. Don't speak unless spoken to. Answer all questions honestly. No human is ever allowed into a Council Meeting. Not even as a witness. Not even if their child is on trial.

"What happens if someone is found guilty by the Council?" Jacob whispered.

"Jacob, that won't happen." Emilia slipped her hand into his.

"But if it does, what could they do to me?"

Emilia shifted in her seat, leaning closer to Jacob's ear. "For minor offenses, the Council can give fines or, in some cases, forced services for the benefit of Magickind. Helping to clean preserves, things like that. For more serious things, they can bind your powers. Make you a *Demadais* and banish you from magical society. No witch or wizard is allowed to speak to anyone who has been stripped of their powers. *Demadaies* have to live as humans for the remainder of their lives. It's different for creatures. The sentient ones rule themselves."

"But what if you're accused of something really serious?"

"Then they give you a choice of life imprisonment or death. There are two dungeons in the United States, but only the Council knows where they are. Honestly, most people just choose death."

"How do they kill you?"

Emilia sat quietly for a moment. "They don't. They make you do it yourself."

Jacob's stomach jolted. For a moment, he thought it was the shock of the idea of the Council offering him life imprisonment or suicide. Then he realized Emilia had reacted to the jolt, too.

The plane rumbled.

Emilia squeezed his hand. "Turbulence. Don't worry, this happens all the time."

Jacob squeezed Emilia's hand back. Maybe it was worth being on a shaky plane if he could hold Emilia's hand this tight.

With a *ding*, the fasten seatbelt light came on. The rumbling worsened. Anxious chatter filled the cabin. A small child near the back of the plane began to cry.

Aunt Iz woke with a start.

"It's ok—" Emilia began.

"No." Iz unbuckled her seatbelt to get up.

"Aunt Iz, the fasten seatbelt light's on because of the turbulence." Emilia tried to coax her back into her seat.

"This isn't an air pocket, Emilia. This is magic. Someone on the plane is causing this."

Panic froze Jacob's veins. "Is it me?"

What if he did it again? What if he broke all the windows? He would kill everyone on the plane. Everyone around him would be sucked out into the abyss.

"It's not you." Iz stepped into the aisle. "Someone is doing this on purpose."

"Ma'am," a harassed flight attendant drawled as she bustled up the aisle, "you're gonna need to sit down. The pilot has turned on the fasten seatbelt sign."

"I am afraid this cannot wait. Please get out of my way." Aunt Iz tried to move past the woman.

The flight attendant planted herself directly in front of Iz, refusing to budge. "Federal Aviation Regulation states—"

"I need my medication." Iz pushed past the woman toward the cockpit.

With a gasp, Iz grabbed the seatback in front of her and collapsed to the floor. Jacob tried to squeeze past Emilia to help Iz, but Emilia wouldn't let him through. The attendant rushed to Iz, calling for the other flight attendants to help.

As soon as the last attendant was focused on Iz, Emilia grabbed Jacob's arm and whispered, "Stay here and make sure they don't leave her."

Jacob didn't want to stay, standing helplessly hunched over his seat with his head banging on the low ceiling every time the plane dropped. He wanted to help Iz, who apparently couldn't breathe, or find whoever wanted to take down the plane, but Emilia was already gone.

17

THE NAMELESS MARTYR

*E*milia tried to think as she moved up the aisle. Iz never took medication. She had lied to give Emilia a chance to save the plane. But how could she find a magic user without doing a location spell people would notice?

She stopped in the aisle next to a man who barked, "The fasten seatbelts light is on for a reason, girlie!" when she bumped into him. But Emilia ignored him and closed her eyes.

She took a breath, willing herself to focus on the flow of energy around her. The engine pulsed electricity into the plane, which shook violently. There was magic in the air, but it was too scattered to follow.

The people she passed tried to calm one another in panicked voices. The plane bounced so badly now no one noticed her grabbing roughly onto their seats as she made her way up the aisle. She kept moving, scanning every face she passed, looking for signs of a spell.

She had almost reached the back of the plane when she felt a burst of energy. Her eyes darted between the passengers surrounding her. It had to be one of them.

On one side, an elderly man grumbled at his pale and wrinkled wife, who looked as though she might be ill. Behind them, a young couple were entwined, kissing one another. None of them could be performing the spell. None of them were concentrating on the plane.

All the other passengers near her were glancing around nervously, talking to their companions, and tightening their seatbelts.

The plane lurched harder than ever, throwing Emilia headfirst into an armrest. Something hot trickled down her nose. Emilia pushed herself up, struggling back to her feet as she wiped blood away from her eyes. The armrest she had hit her head on was slicked with red. The plane shook again. She stumbled and grabbed the shoulder of the armrest's owner, coating him in her blood.

"I'm so sorry," Emilia said.

The man hadn't seemed to notice the blood she'd smeared on his bare arm. He smiled as he listened to music through his headphones, swaying to a rhythm only he could hear. A dragon tattoo wrapped down the man's neck from his cheek to his chest. Emilia stumbled backward, fighting the urge to run away.

"I love you, baby. From now till the end of forever, I'll love you." The couple behind the man professed their undying love for each other, but Emilia concentrated on the man's voice.

"*Navista obitum. Rexhibeo omnis grexa.*"

He was chanting a spell. Speaking calmly, with a smile on his face.

The plane shook violently, sending luggage tumbling into the aisle and oxygen masks falling from the ceiling. Lights flickered overhead. In the front of the plane, someone started to shout the *Lord's Prayer*.

"*Fulguratus!*" Emilia shouted, no longer caring if anyone noticed her magic. She threw the lightning shard into the phone in his hands, then watched as the energy from her strike streaked up the wires, through the headphones, and into the man's ears.

He screamed and scraped at his ears, but his headphones were melting down his face like lava, burning a path through the dragon tattoo.

"Oh God!" someone shouted from behind her. People had turned to stare at her and the man. The smell of burning flesh and plastic mixed with the scent of Emilia's blood. The elderly man's wife vomited onto his lap.

"I think lightning struck the plane," Emilia said, trying to avoid the eyes of everyone around her. "He needs help."

Emilia ran back up the aisle, leaving the man screaming in agony behind her. Her legs shook so badly she didn't notice the plane was flying normally again. As she slid into her seat, one of the passengers in the back of the plane called for someone to help the man with the dragon tattoo, screaming about lightning striking the plane, but no one shouted to bring back the girl who had hurt him. No one understood what they had seen. Emilia turned her face to Jacob, trying to hide the gash on her head from her fellow passengers without leaving blood on Jacob's chest.

"Emi." Jacob tilted her chin up so he could see where she had been hurt.

"I'm fine." She put her head back down just in time as the flight attendant helped Iz back into her seat.

The pilot came over the loud speaker as Iz fastened her seatbelt. "Ladies and gentlemen, I apologize for the unexpected turbulence, but we seem to be all right now. You may remove your masks. We have requested to be moved up in the landing order and should be setting down in New York in just a few minutes."

Emilia tried to staunch the bleeding, hoping it looked like she was covering her face to cry. But as Iz thanked the flight attendant for her help, a drop of blood fell from Emilia's hands onto her unfortunately pale pink shirt.

The flight attendant reached for Emilia and tugged at her hand. "Miss, are you injured?"

Emilia kept her face turned away, but her palm was slicked with blood.

"Miss, you require first ai—" The flight attendant stopped as Iz gently touched her wrist.

"*Immemoris,*" murmured Aunt Iz.

The flight attendant relaxed, and her eyes glazed over.

"Nonsense." Iz patted the flight attendant's hand. "This girl is perfectly fine. She just spilled her drink. However, I would appreciate your giving us several moist towelettes."

The flight attendant turned slowly and walked away.

"Let me see, Emilia," Iz said.

Emilia turned, still trying to keep her face out of view of the other passengers.

"*Pelluere,*" Iz whispered.

Emilia gasped through her teeth as the spell took effect.

She turned back to Jacob when the attendant returned with the moist towelettes.

"Here you go, and don't forget to keep your seatbelt fastened. We're gonna be landing soon," the woman said with a huge smile.

"Is she okay?" Jacob asked.

"She'll be fine." Iz unwrapped a towelette for Emilia.

Emilia took the sweet smelling cloth, trying to clean her hands. "Memory spells can have a few undesirable, temporary side effects."

Iz reached into her purse and pulled out a small, silver-backed mirror. "All this excitement. I think I need to powder my nose."

"Skry," Emilia murmured as Jacob stared after Aunt Iz. "MAGI would be my guess."

No one stopped Iz when she left for the toilet. The flight attendants were too busy looking after the man with the dragon tattoo, except for the one Iz had used a spell on. She was sound asleep in her seat at the front of the plane.

"Here." Jacob opened a packet and began to clean Emilia's face.

She touched the place where the cut had been. The skin on her forehead had knit perfectly back together. The problem was her shirt. More blood had trickled onto it, leaving stains too big to hide.

Jacob took all of the bloody wipes and put them in his waxy paper airsick bag before struggling out of his sweater. "Cover the blood."

"Thanks." Emilia slid into the sweater. It felt warm and cozy, two things that didn't mesh with the last few minutes of her life.

"Thanks for keeping us alive." Jacob squeezed her hand.

Fire trucks and ambulances surrounded the runway where the airplane landed. The first passenger off the plane was the man with the dragon tattoo. He was moaning, barely conscious as the paramedics wheeled him down the aisle.

"I don't feel guilty," Emilia said, hanging on to Jacob's hand, fighting the fear that someone would try to tear her away. "Is that bad? I just destroyed a man's ears. There's only so much magic can heal. Spell damage like that, I don't think he'll ever be able to hear again. And I don't regret it."

"You saved us, Emi. You shouldn't feel guilty for doing what you had to."

Emilia held her breath and tried not to be sick at the sight of the plastic still melted to the man's neck.

"The real pity," Iz said, "is that the police will never arrest him. Even if they knew he was responsible, they could never prove it. MAGI is sending representatives over to the hospital. We can only hope they get there before the Dragons try to rescue their comrade. Although I'm not sure it should really be called a rescue. Going back to a group like that after a failed mission must be very unpleasant."

As they made their way through the crowds to baggage claim, Emilia couldn't help scanning the faces of everyone passing by.

Would the Dragons send someone else after them? Jacob's arm brushed Emilia's as they walked, and somehow feeling him next to her eased her panic.

"But if he had taken down the plane, wouldn't he have died, too?" Jacob whispered while they waited for their bags. "Could a spell save you from that?"

"No," Iz said. "The leader of the Dragons must be a very persuasive person to convince him he should be a martyr and not even be allowed the credit."

"Huh?" Jacob asked.

Iz's phone buzzed. "Ah, Samuel is here. We can finish our conversation in private." She led them out the doors to where Samuel waited with the black BMW.

"Nice to see you all," he said, and though he seemed at ease, Emilia followed his gaze as it roamed over each of them in turn, searching them for signs of damage.

Once they had all climbed into the car and Samuel had pulled out into traffic, Iz resumed her explanation. "You see, Jacob, it is too much of a coincidence that a Dragon tried to crash the plane we, or much more importantly you, were on. If that man had been successful, the Council of Elders and MAGI would have blamed you. They would have had no way of knowing there were, in fact, four wizards on the plane. You would have been branded a killer and made an honored martyr for the Dragons, which means the man who actually destroyed the plane would never have been discovered by MAGI or celebrated by the Dragons."

"But how did they know which plane we were on?" Emilia asked. "You only booked the tickets a few hours ago."

"Someone told them," Samuel said from the front seat. "Someone with access to that sort of information. It could be a Council member, or a MAGI agent, or a friend someone in the family spoke to."

"So really all we know is that we can't trust anyone. Great."

Emilia pulled off Jacob's sweater. She started a cleaning spell, removing the blood from her shirt.

"There are people we can and must trust," Iz said. "If we stop communicating with our allies, we will be alone and more vulnerable than we have ever been before. We simply need to be much more selective. The most important thing is to get Jacob through his trial tomorrow. After that, we will turn our attention to these terrorists."

Terrorists. That sounded right.

"For now, Samuel and I will leave you two to enjoy yourselves for the rest of the day. Please be home by ten o'clock. Jacob has a very long day tomorrow."

"What? Is that safe?" Emilia asked. "If there are people trying to get Jacob, they need to do it before tomorrow. Shouldn't we stay with you?"

"No. Samuel and I are going to the house to redo all the safety enchantments and make sure no one has been there who should not have been. Then I will meet with some friends from MAGI. I have also instructed the professor to bring the rest of the household here. It would be best if we were all together."

Emilia started to protest again.

"But not," Iz interrupted, "until the house is secure. I don't want either of you there until everything is ready, and since we don't know who else to trust, there is no other safe house for you to go to. The safest thing for you to do is disappear into the crowds of the city. Do not use any magic, and no one will be able to find you. No one knows you are going to be roaming the city except Samuel and me."

Emilia nodded. "What about you?"

"Samuel and I will take care of each other," Iz said as Samuel pulled over on 5th Avenue in front of a large department store. "Stay together, and try to enjoy the day. In times as uncertain as these, we must find joy and freedom whenever we can."

Emilia pulled Jacob out of the car.

Iz pressed a clip of bills into Emilia's hand.

"Thanks, Aunt Iz," Emilia said.

"Call if you need me," Samuel said.

And with that, Jacob and Emilia were alone in the Big Apple.

18

CITY THAT NEVER SLEEPS

*N*othing had prepared Jacob for New York City.

Chaos of a kind he had never seen before surrounded him. Thousands of people passed each other on the streets, going about their different lives. The lilt of so many different languages touched his ears Jacob lost count, but two words were on almost everyone's lips.

Airplane. Dam.

The police on the corner were talking about it, sitting high above the crowd on their horses, trading theories on what they thought had happened to the dam. But none of them looked at Jacob. No one suspected he had flown on the ill-fated plane to New York to stand trial for the deaths at the Neversink Dam. Or that the malfunctioning airplane that had landed so close to the city had been his fault as well.

Emilia steered him through the crowds to show him the best of the city. She took him to the park and for frozen hot chocolate. He watched her coo as she gazed into windows whose displays danced with diamonds.

A pain burned in Jacob's chest. She was trying to give him a perfect day. In case it was their last.

Aunt Iz's New York home was a brick townhouse on the Upper West Side. The lights inside blazed bright, and Samuel met them at the cab when they arrived.

"How do you like New York, Jacob?" A strained look filled Samuel's eyes as he led them up the front steps.

"It was great." A sense of dread settled into Jacob's stomach.

"Samuel, are you all right?" Emilia asked.

"I'm fine, Emilia. Larkin and Stone are here. We've been discussing recent events." Samuel ushered them into the house.

Recent events seemed like a strange way of saying *that time when a band of vicious killers tried to frame you for crashing a plane, and oh right, they tried to kill you, your best friend, and the closest thing to a parent you have.* Jacob laughed to himself, and Emilia arched her eyebrow quizzically.

"Don't worry about it," Jacob muttered.

The house wasn't as big as the Mansion House, but it was by no means small. It had the same homey, yet elegant feel Iz seemed to favor.

Emilia started down the long, carpeted hall beside the staircase.

"Where are you going?" Samuel stepped in front of Emilia.

"To the dining room to see Larkin."

"You can't go in there, Emilia. They're having an important meeting, and it can't be interrupted," Samuel said. "Why don't you show Jacob where he'll be sleeping? Molly hasn't arrived with the others yet, so he can have first pick of the guest rooms."

"What sort of important meeting can't we go to?" Emilia scowled. "The trial tomorrow is for Jacob. He has a right to know what they're saying, and I want to go with him."

"Sorry." Samuel shook his head. "Iz told me that if you said that, I had to tell you there are some things Jacob can't know tomorrow. If he knew them and some of the Council members found out, it would only make things much worse for him. Jacob is safer not knowing, which means you can't know either."

Emilia glared at Samuel, her fists clenched Jacob almost expected to see steam blossom from her ears.

"Fine," she sighed finally.

Emilia turned without another word and stalked up the stairs.

Jacob gave Samuel an apologetic smile before following her.

Emilia walked up two flights of stairs and into a bedroom that had to be hers. It smelled like lilacs and had a wonderful view of the old brick houses across the street. Both of their suitcases waited on her bed.

"You can choose whichever room you want." She handed Jacob his suitcase.

Jacob took his bag to the room next door and dropped it onto the bed without even turning on the lights. He really didn't care where he slept. He just wanted to get back to Emilia. He was in her room again in less than thirty seconds. Even that short time away had made it hard to breathe. She was like an anti-anxiety pill.

Emilia handed him the golden folder from the plane. Jacob settled into a comfortable chair in the corner to reread all the information he could apparently be allowed.

"How are you doing it?" Emilia asked.

Jacob set the folder on the floor. She had curled up on the windowsill. She looked almost like the Emilia he used to know. The small one who used to sit beside him as they gazed at stars for hours.

"How are you calm? You've only known about all of this for a few weeks. But you're fine. We were attacked and almost killed on a plane. And you're fine." Her voice cracked. She hid her face behind the thick black veil of her hair.

Jacob walked over and sat beside her. He thought for a moment, gazing at the New York skyline. "I'm not fine." He pushed the hair away from Emilia's face, tucking the strands behind her ear. "I'm terrified. But I am going to go in front of that

Council tomorrow, because if that's what it takes to be a part of your"—he stopped himself—"this world, it's worth it."

Emilia smiled and pressed his palm to her cheek. "Always worth it."

~

$\mathcal{J}$acob and Emilia studied the C.O.E. file together late into the night. They heard Molly arrive with Claire and Connor, but no one interrupted them or came to tell them to go to sleep. Emilia's phone buzzed several times before she turned it off and put it out of sight under her pillow. Dexter would not like being ignored.

Jacob didn't know what time they finally fell asleep, Emilia curled at the head of her bed while Jacob slumbered in the comfy chair. When morning came, Molly knocked on the door, summoning them both down to breakfast. Emilia led Jacob to the dining room, where Aunt Iz was already eating. There was no sign of the MAGI agents.

"Where's Larkin?" Emilia asked as she sat down at the table.

"She and Stone left late last night." Aunt Iz passed Emilia a plate of eggs. "The man from the plane disappeared from the hospital before MAGI arrived. They joined the group looking for him this morning. She wanted me to tell you she is very sorry she didn't get to see you this time, but she will call you this week and visit as soon as she can."

Jacob's stomach tightened. The man who had tried to kill them was out there again. As easy as that. And Jacob was the one standing trial.

"I am sorry I was not able to talk you through more of the information in the file last night," Iz said, wrinkles forming between her silver eyebrows.

"I'm fine. Emilia and I spent hours going over everything."

"Good." Iz smiled. "Eat quickly and go get dressed. We have to leave in one hour. The Proctor House is all the way across town, and traffic will be a nightmare."

"I'm coming, too." Emilia looked at Iz sideways as she ate her eggs, as though daring her to say no.

"Normally, I would say no, but as that would only result in your taking a cab across town by yourself and attempting to sneak into the Proctor House, I suppose you may come. You will not be allowed into the meeting, of course." Iz stood. "And remember, you must hold your tongue and be polite, for Jacob's sake as well as your own."

"I will be the sweetest angel!" Emilia called after her.

19

THE COUNCIL OF ELDERS

*A*n hour later, Jacob found himself in a car making its way across Manhattan. He wore charcoal grey slacks and a deep blue shirt. Claire had pinned a pink note to the shirt.

The blue will make you look grown up and responsible. It also complements your eyes. Don't argue, just get dressed.

You can do this.

Kisses,

Claire

They drove past stately stone homes and massive buildings. The number of people the city contained still amazed Jacob.

Samuel navigated the car onto a road that cut through Central Park.

The strangeness of driving past groves of trees with skyscrapers peeping over the tops sent Jacob's head spinning.

They arrived at the Proctor House on the Upper East Side where a tall man in a dark suit waited outside.

"Ms. Gray." He nodded as Aunt Iz led them into the house.

There were still a few minutes left until Jacob's appointment time, but the buzzing of voices already drifted down the hall.

"Ah, Isadora!" An elderly man bustled toward them. Rather

cheerful looking, the man had a large belly and a red face. He had no hair on top, but out of both sides of his head grew long white curls.

"Orem," Iz said with a smile, "it is lovely to see you again."

Orem kissed Iz on the cheek. "Emilia, you have grown!" He laughed, taking both of Emilia's hands and holding them out to the sides so he could get a better look at her. "Sometimes I cannot believe how quickly the years pass."

"Mr. Proctor, this is Jacob," Emilia said.

Mr. Proctor's smile faded when he turned to Jacob. "Yes, well, I can't really say it is a pleasure to meet you. Not under these circumstances, at any rate. You should go wait in the study. They'll call you when it's time."

"I'll go with you." Emilia slipped her arm through Jacob's elbow and began to lead him away.

Mr. Proctor made a faint grumbling noise.

"Just for the wait, not the meeting," Emilia reassured him with her most winning smile as she walked Jacob down the hall to the study.

It wasn't like Aunt Iz's or Professor Eames's studies at all. This study had books, but they were only on one wall. The other walls were covered in glass cases. One of the cases displayed a sword with a sign that said it had been used by one of the greatest dragon hunters of the sixteenth century. There was a manifest from the prison in Salem where accused witches awaiting trial had been kept, a wand that had been the talisman of the first head of the Proctor Clan, and dozens of other magical artifacts.

In the center of the room rested a large and ornately carved desk. The placard on the front read *Marshal Orem Proctor, C.O.E.*

Emilia pushed the placard aside and perched on the desk's embossed leather surface. "Mr. Proctor doesn't care so much about actual magic as he does seeming important. His family was almost removed from the Council altogether when I was little. Ever since, he's been desperate to hold on to his Council seat."

Jacob gazed up at a large painting of Merlin hovering majestically over a mist-covered lake. "What happened to get him removed? I thought the Council was a forever thing." He peered into a case that held a silver knife with a tag that read *Sacrificial knife used by Aztec wizards. Note: Generally the sacrifices were of Magickind, as their blood was thought to be more potent and pleasing to the gods.*

Jacob swallowed hard, trying to push air past the knot in his throat. He didn't want to think about wizard sacrifices. Panic surged through him again. He sat by Emilia, clenching his fists so she wouldn't notice his trembling hands.

Emilia glanced at the open doorway. "He was grooming his nephew as his heir, but the stupid kid got greedy. He went to the Hag for help."

"Hag?" Jacob asked.

"All you need to know is Iz doesn't really like him," Emilia said, "and he doesn't always like her from what she says. But he always pretends they're the best of friends whenever they see each other."

"Why doesn't Iz like him?"

"She says he has no morals. He'll do whatever it takes to hold on to his seat on the Council. It doesn't matter if it's right or wrong as long as it keeps him in power." Emilia took Jacob's hand. "Don't think he'll be friendly in there. He'll treat you however he thinks will please the majority of the people in the room."

Jacob nodded. His mouth had suddenly gone too dry to speak.

A woman cleared her throat loudly behind them. "Please follow me, Mr. Evans. Ms. Gray, if you wish to have lunch, there is food available in the kitchen."

"I just ate," Emilia said.

"There is food in the kitchen. You may eat or not, but you will wait there." The woman left the room, and Jacob followed her, waving lamely at Emilia as he went.

"Sit." The woman pointed to a wooden chair opposite a large set of double doors. The doors were carved wood, but unlike those at the Mansion House, these seemed heavy. Everything at the Mansion House breathed life, but walking through these doors could lead Jacob to a dungeon. Or death. The woman swung one of the dark doors open and entered the room, leaving him alone in the hall.

Jacob waited outside the meeting room. He didn't want to sit. He wanted to run for his life, or at the very least, pace the long hallway. But he sat, too afraid his legs might give out if he tried to stand.

He kept going over key phrases in his head. Points Emilia had told him he needed to make to the Council, if they gave him the chance, which she said wasn't very likely.

Finally, the door opened and an elderly man beckoned him in. He suddenly felt as though the wait had been too short and he needed more time to prepare. But it was no good. The old man waited for him to follow.

Somehow his legs carried him into the room. If he hadn't been so nervous, he might have appreciated the beauty of the large dining room, adorned with rich red and gold wallpaper. Three elegant crystal chandeliers hung from the ceiling, and a long mahogany dining room table stood in the center of the room.

The witches and wizards at the table were all seated facing him. Jacob felt like he had walked into a painting of The Last Supper.

He looked up and down the table. Iz sat to the far left. She gave Jacob a small smile. There were ten other wizards in all, eleven counting the elderly gentleman wheezing behind him. This was wrong. The C.O.E. folder had specifically said thirteen Clan Heads and one scribe. There should be fourteen people sitting at the table waiting to judge him. Two Clan heads were missing.

The elderly gentleman who had shown him into the room shuffled back to his place at one end of the long table where a laptop sat open, waiting for him. Mr. Proctor sat at the other end of the table. According to Council rules, the representative of the Clan whose house they were meeting in had the right to preside over the Council meeting, which meant Mr. Proctor would be in charge of his trial.

"Jacob Evans, you have been summoned before the Council to discuss the incident that took place at Fairfield High School." Mr. Proctor studied a sheet of paper on the table. "You have been accused of rebel behavior. Namely, performing magic in front of non-magic people and causing property damage in excess of thirty-seven thousand dollars and injury to over one hundred people. These charges are very serious. Please explain your actions."

Jacob opened his mouth to speak, but words wouldn't come. "Umm...wha...I." He looked to Aunt Iz, who raised her shoulders and took a deep, exaggerated breath. Jacob nodded and followed suit.

"I was at school when the principal called me to his office. He —" Jacob didn't want to relive this in front of these people, but there was no other choice. "He came to tell me my father had died. Then before I knew it, all the windows exploded."

"As simple as that?" a dark-haired man to Jacob's left asked. "Are you denying you caused the damage?"

"No," Jacob said quickly. "It was me, but I didn't know it at the time. I didn't know what I was capable of."

"Can you describe how you felt when it happened?" asked a woman with dyed black hair and far too much makeup. Jacob almost didn't answer he was so fascinated by her overly arched, painted-on eyebrows.

"I felt," Jacob said, pulling his gaze away from the woman's face, "like everything inside shut down for a second. I couldn't breathe or think. There was this anger and pain that started to swell in the back of my brain—and then it happened."

"Why anger?" a little man asked.

"My father and I didn't really get along. He was gone all the time, and I felt like he didn't care. When the principal told me he was dead, I guess I knew he was gone for good, and my father still probably wouldn't have cared."

"I think that is a very understandable reaction," the black-haired, too-much-makeup woman said. "Though I could never condone destruction, I can easily believe it was accidental."

A few of the other Council members nodded in assent.

"But that was not the first time you did magic, was it, Mr. Evans?" the dark-haired man asked.

"Mr. Wayland," Aunt Iz said with a hint of warning in her tone.

The man's dark hair and chiseled face left no doubt in Jacob's mind that he was Dexter's father.

"The other incident to which you are referring was reported to the Council immediately after it happened, and that was years ago," Iz said. "No one was harmed, and Mr. Evans had no idea what had happened."

"But Mr. Evans seems to be very clever. How do we know he didn't realize he had extraordinary abilities then?" Mr. Wayland asked.

"I didn't," Jacob rushed to say. He could feel the tide in the room turning, and not in his favor. "I didn't know anything."

"Emilia Gray didn't tell you anything?" the pointy-looking witch who had sent Emilia to the kitchen asked.

"Let me answer that, Mr. Evans," Aunt Iz said. "Emilia Gray is my ward. She came to me immediately following the incident. Council procedure was thereafter followed to the letter. As with all first manifestations of magic, communication was severed until after the second incident at Fairfield High School."

"It is not your place to answer questions for the person standing trial," Mr. Wayland snapped.

"Nor is it the purpose of this Council meeting to question the conduct of my ward," Aunt Iz said without even looking at Mr. Wayland. "It is common for two displays of magic to occur before a wizard is accepted as a member of Magickind. Are we here because Jacob's display was one of extraordinary power, or because the Dragons, whom he has never had contact with, are trying to twist a young boy's grief into something sinister?"

"Mr. Evans," Mr. Proctor's voice rose unnecessarily as though he were yelling over a fight, "will you attest that you were unaware of any magic involving Emilia Gray, that you were unaware of any of your magical capabilities at the time of the Fairfield High School incident, and that the Fairfield High School incident was in fact unintentional and the result of extreme emotional distress?"

"Yes," Jacob said, amazed he could actually make a sound.

"Then I think it is time for a vote."

"What about the incident on the plane yesterday?" a skeletal man to his left asked, staring at a paper in front of him. "MAGI states that all one hundred seven people aboard were in danger. Including you, Ms. Gray. Certainly, yesterday you were aware you are a wizard, Mr. Evans."

Mr. Proctor riffled through the sheets of paper in front of him. "I have no listing of such an incident being under consideration for this trial."

"That is because it is not a part of this trial," Iz said. "But I thank you, Mr. Chandler, for being so careful to ensure the Council has full awareness of all pending issues." She nodded to Mr. Chandler. "I myself was planning to bring the matter to the Council's attention at a more appropriate time."

"If this boy almost caused a plane to crash, it should most certainly be part of this trial, which is primarily about the use of destructive magic in front of humans." Mr. Wayland pounded his fist on the table.

"Yes, of course. But Jacob was not the cause of the incident on the plane. He was very nearly the victim of it."

Murmurs spread around the table.

"I have a full file of evidence from MAGI that proves it was not Jacob who endangered the plane, but rather a Dragon assassin," Aunt Iz said. "MAGI has pulled security footage from several cameras in the airport that clearly show the man being wheeled into an ambulance."

"An ambulance?" Mr. Proctor mopped the beads of sweat from his forehead with a silk handkerchief. "But if he was the one doing the attacking—"

"Emilia and I were on the plane as well."

"Emilia who?" said the man at the laptop.

"You know very well I mean Emilia Gray, Mr. Ogden," Iz snapped. "When we became aware the plane was, in fact, being attacked by magic, we stopped the attacker. It was quite gruesome. Emilia melted the man's headphones right into his ears. The smell was repugnant."

"If Emilia did magic in front of humans, she should stand trial as well." The bony man tapped the table with his withered finger.

"Emilia who?" Mr. Ogden asked again.

"For God's sake, Emilia Gray, you idiot," Mr. Wayland shouted.

"Emilia Gray should not stand trial for saving over a hundred people!" a very wrinkled woman said. "Did the humans notice anything?"

"Yes," Iz said. "But as they were all fearing for their lives at that moment, I'm sure none of the other passengers will be reporting anything unusual. After all, who would believe them?"

"They could report it," Mr. Chandler spat. "Just because it was your ward who performed the magic—"

Iz's knuckles turned white as she clutched the edge of the

table. "MAGI is monitoring the passengers closely to be sure none of them talk. If they do, memory spells can and will be performed to mitigate any damaging memories."

"And how is it that you alone have all this information from MAGI?" Mr. Wayland asked, standing up and pointing at Iz.

Jacob wanted to stop Mr. Wayland and defend Iz. But his body seemed to have forgotten how to move.

"Are the Gray pockets that deep?" Mr. Wayland asked. "Do you own MAGI?"

"I have information you do not because I am willing to ask. Because I am willing to listen to what MAGI has to say instead of getting my information from far less reputable sources that do not have the best interests of Magickind in mind." Iz pulled a file from her bag and slapped it down on the table. "I have evidence proving the incident was but a small part of a plot by the Dragons, and that the plot goes much deeper than one plane crash."

"That sort of information should not be bandied about in front of a person standing trial, Isadora," Mr. Proctor sputtered.

"Precisely, Mr. Proctor. So let us take a vote on Mr. Evans's case and move on to matters of real significance concerning the safety not only of Magickind but of humans as well."

Jacob wasn't sure if Iz was right to push for a vote so soon. So many of the Council members were glaring at him. He didn't know if he could win. And Mr. Wayland would definitely send him to a dungeon if he got the chance.

"Fine," Mr. Proctor growled. "I hereby ask the Council to vote on the matter of Jacob Evans. All those who think Mr. Evans is guilty of rebellious acts endangering Magickind, raise your hand and say *aye*."

Mr. Chandler and the woman who had brought Jacob to wait outside both raised their hands instantly, along with Mr. Wayland. "Aye," their voices chorused.

A pudgy witch in the corner also raised her hand. "Aye"

Mr. Proctor looked around.

Jacob was sure if one more Council member raised their hand, Mr. Proctor would, too. Emilia had been right. He wanted to be on the winning side, no matter whose life would be destroyed as a result.

The room had gone quiet. Mr. Proctor's left eye started to twitch. "Is that all for the ayes?" he asked, sounding like a child who'd had his toy taken away. "Those who think Mr. Evans is not guilty, raise your hand and say *nay*."

Aunt Iz's hand was first in the air, followed quickly by five others.

Mr. Proctor raised his hand last. "The nays have it. Jacob Evans, you are hereby cleared of all charges. Please leave the room. The Council has important matters to discuss." He flapped his hand dramatically at the door, shooing Jacob out.

Jacob pushed himself to his feet, hardly believing it could be over so quickly. "Thank you," he said as he half-ran to the door. He had almost made it into the hall when he heard a voice behind him.

"Mr. Evans." Mr. Wayland's voice dripped with malice. "In the future, I suggest you try to avoid any actions that might bring you back in front of the Council. Remember where exactly you stand within Magickind and don't cross your boundaries and meddle in things in which you have no rightful part. Should you ever be brought in front of the Council again, I doubt you will find us so generous."

"Right," Jacob said. "I do appreciate your generosity, Mr. Wayland." He slipped into the hallway, pulling the door shut behind him.

Immediately, pounding footsteps raced toward him. He turned just in time to see a blur of black hair before Emilia threw herself at him. Jacob wrapped his arms around her. He wasn't going to the dungeons.

Emilia shook in his arms. Her tears fell on Jacob's shoulder.

"Shh. It's okay, Emi." He pressed his cheek to her hair. "They voted not guilty."

"I know." Emilia hiccupped. "But they were being so awful, I thought..." A new wave of tears sent her back to Jacob's shoulder.

"How do you know what they said?"

"Come on." Emilia wiped her cheeks and dragged him down the hallway.

"Where are we going?" Jacob asked.

"To listen to the meeting."

"But I just managed to not get sent to the dungeons, and they sent me out here so I wouldn't hear what they're talking about."

"Jacob, someone is trying to kill us, or more particularly, you. Don't you want to know why?"

Jacob didn't answer. He had been so happy about the trial being over he had almost forgotten the whole attempted murder thing.

"Come on, and be quiet."

20

THE TIPPING POINT

*E*milia pulled Jacob through the crisp, white kitchen, which had either never been used, or was cleaned with a liberal amount of bleach several times a day. She pushed through a narrow door in the corner of the room into a small pantry.

Emilia turned sideways and pulled Jacob in behind her. "Close the door," she whispered.

The door clicked quietly shut. The only light came from a small air vent at the very bottom of the back wall. "What are we doing in here?"

Emilia reached into her back pocket and pulled out a tiny mirror. "Not getting caught. *Volavertus*." The mirror shimmered for a moment, casting strange shadows onto the pantry walls, before voices sounded from the depths of its glowing surface.

"The time has come for action."

"I think that's Mr. Chandler," Emilia murmured, holding the mirror up close to her ear.

"We can no longer be driven from our homes and forced into hiding. Now is when we must act. It is time to show the humans who they are stealing from. To show them the consequences of their actions and prove we will take retribution."

"What are you doing?" Jacob asked, his eyes flicking from Emilia to the mirror.

"I snuck a mirror into Iz's purse on our way in." Emilia smiled. "You don't think Claire's the only trouble maker in the family?"

"But Iz never accepted—"

"Shh," Emilia hushed him. "My mirror to my mirror. No acceptance needed. Now listen."

"Are you mad, Mr. Chandler? Or perhaps I misunderstood." Aunt Iz spoke calmly, but Emilia recognized the danger in her tone. "Are you actually suggesting we reveal ourselves to the world? That we should attack the general population outright?"

"Do you—" Mr. Chandler tried to interrupt, but Iz continued, her voice still calm but louder now.

"If humans discover the existence of our kind, they hunt us."

"Let them try," growled a voice, too softly for Emilia to identify.

"They may not be able to find any real witches, but humans are violent," Iz said, each of her words striking like arrows. "Do you want another massacre like the one at Salem? Those people never found a real witch, but they killed each other. Innocent humans who knew nothing about magic. Some wizards think it doesn't matter. A few human deaths don't bother them. But I believe a human life is just as sacred as a magical one, and I will grieve the loss of either, equally."

"Then you are a fool, Isadora Gray." It was Mr. Wayland who spoke this time. "You would sacrifice the progress of our kind to protect humans, who have proven themselves to be vicious murderers, horrible bigots, and incapable of protecting the planet we have been forced to share with them. We must ensure our own survival, whether or not that is conducive to the survival of humans."

"Mr. Wayland hates humans," Emilia whispered, answering the confused look on Jacob's face. "His territory is crowded, and

MAGI says it's too dangerous for him to expand his land. Dex says his dad thinks the humans have taken too much."

"Are you proposing the Council condone the killing of humans?" a woman's voice asked.

"No," Mr. Wayland said. "I am proposing we let the Dragons follow their course and thank them when they're done. I would never expect this Council to have the courage to do anything significant for the advancement of Magickind."

"The rebels aren't just some fringe group anymore. They are gaining power, and quickly. If they reveal us to the public—" said a woman's raspy voice.

"Ms. Sable, please," a male voice said. "There have always been problems controlling some of the more rebellious young wizards and travelers, but as long as the Clans remain in alliance—"

"The Clans haven't been *in alliance* for a long time," Emilia whispered in Jacob's ear. "If he thinks—"

Iz's voice spoke clearly and firmly through the mirror. "The reports from MAGI have suggested the recent atrocities are not the acts of disgruntled youths, but systematic attacks by a rebel group strong enough to be called an army. These Dragons are a real threat and must be treated as such. Already there have been disappearances. Proteus's daughter Willow disappeared weeks ago."

"What does that have to do with us?" Mr. Wayland snapped.

"Centaurs don't just go missing. There are so few places for them to go. Proteus has heard rumors of wizards on the preserve. Wizards traveling together."

"A group of travelers taking up residence on a preserve is not unheard of," Mr. Proctor said. "And even if there are a few rebellious sorts in the woods somewhere, does that really need to cause this kind of concern?"

"Some of the resources the rebels have—the numbers, the money—are unprecedented for a mere group of travelers," Iz said, her voice steady as the murmurs in the room grew. "They are receiving help from within the Clans. Aiding any group whose aim is to expose our existence is against the very principles upon which this Council was founded, as well as against the laws that govern our kind. Any wizard or Clan found aiding the rebels would be committing an act of war against the rest of the Clans and the Council of Elders.

"Should the situation progress to that point, the international community may also consider involving themselves for the protection of Magickind the world over. If this conflict escalates to an international level, the freedoms we have long enjoyed in America could be lost to us forever."

"Is that true?" Jacob glanced up from the mirror and bumped heads with Emilia.

"Yes," Emilia said, aware for the first time of how close she was to Jacob. Of his hip pressing against hers.

"If the international community sees American wizards standing up and taking their rightful place at the head of society," Mr. Wayland said, his voice rising in excitement, "they will see the Dragons are right in demanding that Magickind be given their due. They will hail the Dragons as leaders and heroes."

"What the Dragons are doing is wrong." Iz's voice rang loud and clear over the angry chatter in the room. "And not all wizards will agree to stand idly by. This could turn into a war between factions of Magickind, as well as a war with the humans. What will this Council do when the human government decides we are a threat and bombs one of the preserves? Whose hands will that blood be on?"

"Humans could destroy us. They would lock us up." The mirror shook in Emilia's hand. "They'd do tests on us. Does Mr. Wayland want Dexter to end up in a padded room?"

Jacob wrapped his hand around hers, helping her hold the mirror steady.

"If the humans are naïve enough to threaten us, then we shall destroy their government," Mr. Chandler spat.

"It is not for us to decide what path their government takes," Iz said.

"But it could be!" Mr. Wayland shouted.

There was silence.

Emilia held her breath.

"I am afraid that is not something my family will ever be a part of, Mr. Wayland," Iz said softly.

"Until such a time as trust can be restored within the Council, I suggest we end this meeting," a man's low rumbling voice said.

"Or until such a time as a new Council has been formed," Mr. Wayland snapped without even a note of apprehension in his voice.

Mr. Proctor sputtered. "That is a treasonous statement. That could constitute a declaration of war."

"So be it," Mr. Wayland said.

The *clomp* of footsteps and the *crash* of a door being flung open carried through the glass.

The relief Emilia had felt at Jacob being declared innocent vanished.

War. They were facing an all-out magical war. Dexter's father wanted it to happen. And she had just heard the beginning of it.

"Jacob," Emilia whispered as she silently pushed Jacob toward the pantry door, "we have to get out of here. Aunt Iz will be looking for us."

Jacob reached for the door, but Emilia stopped him, putting her hand on his chest. His heart raced beneath her palm.

"No one can know what we heard," Emilia said. "Not even Iz."

They emerged into the bright whiteness of the kitchen. Emilia pushed herself up to sit on one of the sparkling counters. Her breath caught in her throat. Tears burned in her eyes. She forced the air from her lungs as a laugh, trying to smile. Trying to look as though the world weren't falling apart.

"You did it, Jacob. You get to come home." Emilia took his hand, holding on to it like a lifeline.

Jacob slid onto the counter next to Emilia. A smile hitched onto his face. Their eyes met. So much had changed since the first time they had sat together at Fairfield Elementary.

At least he's safe, Emilia thought. She squeezed Jacob's hand, and for a moment, his smile became almost real.

Aunt Iz found them in the kitchen and rushed them out the front door and into the waiting car. Samuel's face fell at the sight of Iz's grim expression and Jacob and Emilia's plastered on smiles.

"Oh, Jacob," Samuel said, worry spreading into his eyes. "What did they say?"

"Not guilty," Jacob said.

"Wonderful." Samuel pulled out into traffic. "They had no other choice. No way they could've convicted you."

"Funny," Jacob muttered. "You seemed to think they had convicted me a second ago."

"They'll be glad to hear the good news at the house. Claire and Connor have been calling me all morning wanting to know what's happening." Samuel looked at Jacob through the rear view mirror. "Everything's going to be fine now."

Samuel gave them a smile. A smile Emilia couldn't help noticing didn't quite reach his eyes.

21

BEYOND THE BARRICADE

*A*s soon as the car stopped, Claire burst out the front door, followed closely by Connor. Jacob plastered a smile on his face and climbed out of the car.

"Jacob!" Claire shouted as she launched herself at him with such force he fell back into the car and onto Emilia. "Did they let you off?" she squealed, still locked around him.

"Yep," Jacob choked, barely able to breathe.

Emilia laughed as Claire tried to squirm her way backwards out of the car.

Connor reached in and grasped Jacob's hand. "I knew you'd be okay," Connor said, giving him a back-thumping hug.

"Thanks," Jacob said, distracted by the sight of Molly running down the stairs with tears streaming down her face. She gave him a big kiss on the cheek.

"Everything all right then?" she asked.

"Yep," Jacob said.

"Good." Molly wiped her tears on a kitchen towel. "We'll have a celebration feast in the kitchen."

The three of them marched Jacob into the house, chatting excitedly. Emilia followed closely behind. The professor met them in the hall and gave him a "well done," but never made it to the kitchen. Jacob suspected Iz had pulled Professor Eames and Samuel away to tell them about the Council meeting.

Jacob sat at the table while Claire dished him ice cream and sang silly victory songs she made up on the spot.

You can have chocolate or vanilla because you're a lucky fella.

I'll even add Nutella and a little hot fudge!

Molly bustled about the kitchen baking treats, and Connor asked for a blow-by-blow. Everyone seemed so happy he was safe.

This must be what having a family felt like. A whole house full of people who genuinely cared about what happened to him. And he cared about all of them, too.

Emilia sang along with Claire. She smiled and laughed, but when her eyes met Jacob's, he could sense the fear she couldn't quite hide. He had finally found a family, and now they were all in danger. The knot in his stomach tightened unbearably.

After an hour, Aunt Iz showed up in the kitchen, looking tired but happy. Samuel and Professor Eames were nowhere to be seen. Jacob suspected they were already out doing something for Iz, but the victory celebration continued.

Finally, after Claire curled up under the table, clenching her stomach and declaring her imminent demise from too much ice cream, Molly cleared away the feast, and Jacob escaped to his room to change. He needed quiet to process everything that had happened. He had started unbuttoning his shirt when a quiet knock sounded on the door.

"Jacob," Emilia called from the hallway.

"Come in."

Emilia walked straight over to him and buried her face on his chest. "We can do this, right?"

He held her close. "You and me, we can do anything, Emi."

Emilia laughed a little and stepped away, brushing a tear from her eye. "Iz says to get dressed. She's taking the two of us to see a show to celebrate. It's her New York City tradition. Claire says she packed a theatre outfit, and she doesn't want to hear any arguments."

Emilia had almost reached the door when Jacob had to ask, "And Dexter? Did you get ahold of him? Is he coming?" He hadn't wanted to bring Dexter up, but what sort of a friend would he be if he didn't?

"I tried to call, but he won't answer. I understand he's mad at me, and that's fine. But I wish he were here instead of with his horrible father." Emilia scrubbed her face with her hands. "I just want to find him and tell him the awful things his father said." She took a deep breath and pushed her hair away from her face.

"He'll turn up."

"I know." Emilia gave a halfhearted smile. "You'd better get dressed before Aunt Iz has a fit. Molly's got more food for you in the kitchen when you're ready." The door closed behind her.

As much of a jerk as Dexter had always been to him, Emilia was right. If Mr. Wayland was going to try and break apart the Council of Elders, Dexter should be warned. He had been living with the Grays since the family left Fairfield. Dexter was just as much a Gray as he was a Wayland. If lines were going to be drawn, he should have the chance to choose which side he wanted to be on. And Jacob had no doubt Dexter would choose whichever side of the line kept him with Emilia.

Jacob opened his suitcase and sifted through the clothing for something labeled *theatre*. Sure enough, there was an outfit waiting for him, neatly folded and sealed in a bag. He shook his head. Leave it to Claire to think of packing something like this when he was on his way to a trial. But then, who could have foreseen an assassination attempt on the plane? Or Council members who actually supported the Dragons?

Jacob didn't particularly want to go to the theatre. He wanted to run. Take Emilia and run as far away from the broken Council as possible. Get her away from whatever danger lurked in the shadows. Go someplace nice and quiet where not even magic could reach them.

The outfit Claire had chosen for him didn't make him feel any better. The pants were dark, and the light shirt had a mandarin collar. Jacob didn't care what Claire thought. This was overkill. He sat on the kitchen counter eating a sandwich and feeling ridiculous. He looked like he should be in a magazine. Well, except for the sandwich part.

"Are you ready?" Emilia asked as she walked into the kitchen. She stole a piece of chicken that had fallen out of Jacob's sandwich and onto his plate, oblivious to his enamored stares. She had pinned up her hair to display her delicate, dangling silver earrings. She wore a light blue chiffon dress that whispered every time she moved. She pulled on a cream sweater that matched the color of his shirt perfectly.

Jacob made a mental note to stop arguing when Claire dressed him. The girl obviously knew what she was doing.

◊

*J*acob had never seen a musical before, let alone a Broadway show. His school had done shows every year, but when finding food required constant work, the school play had never seemed important.

Iz insisted that being introduced to Broadway was a delicate procedure. A person only had one chance to see their first Broadway show, so it had to be a good one. Preferably a classic.

As they sped downtown in a bright yellow cab, Iz's face beamed while she explained the intricacies of musical theatre, but Jacob was too busy wondering where Samuel was. Where had he gone to make riding in a cab necessary? Jacob smiled and nodded but didn't really catch much of Iz's explanation of the important meaning in this particular show.

They climbed out of the cab next to the theatre and joined the lines of people waiting to be directed to their seats.

The theatre was as close to a fairyland as Jacob could imagine any building outside Aunt Iz's domain to be. Chandeliers cast their glistening light onto the patrons below. Red velvet curtains draped the stage, hiding the promise of the story within. Emilia pulled Jacob into his seat as the orchestra began tuning their instruments, searching for the perfect pitch to create their music.

Jacob's mind was still racing when the lights in the theatre dimmed. Then the show began, and it touched everything he felt inside.

The mother who sent her child away, hoping she would find a better life. The evil policeman bent on upholding the law, regardless of why the crimes were committed. The young people willing to fight and die to create a new world, a better world filled with the hope of equality for all people. A heartbroken girl dying for a man who couldn't even see how much she cared. Young lovers who wanted nothing more than to stay with each other but had to risk eternal separation to fight for a new life.

As the young fighters built a barricade, trying to find a way to survive the coming battle, Jacob couldn't help but wonder who in the story he would be. If a battle did come, which side of the barricade would he be on? Which side was the right side? Was he the heartbroken lover destined to never be loved in return, or was he the hero risking everything to protect the girl he loved? And most importantly, was protecting a secret worth all this blood? Was salvaging the Council worth being a part of the fight for a better future? Would it be better to wait it out someplace quiet and see who was left standing when the whole thing was over?

The young men on stage fell on the barricade, dying for their cause. Trying to create a new world they would never see. What did it look like when wizards killed each other? Did a dead wizard look different from a dead human?

As a small boy was killed onstage, Emilia reached over to hold his hand. She laced her fingers through his. Tears streamed silently down her cheeks.

Yes. Samuel was right. The fight would be worth it. If there were a way to protect Emilia, he would do it. Because he loved her. And as afraid as he might be of the fight to come, it was nothing compared to the fear of losing her. He would do whatever he could to keep Magickind from being discovered. He would fight the rebels. He really had no choice.

Jacob squeezed Emilia's hand and she squeezed back, and for that moment in a darkened theatre, she was his.

The show ended, and Jacob stood to clap with the rest of the audience. The crowd exited the theatre in a pack, all happily chattering about the wonderful performance.

"I have always loved that show," Aunt Iz said as they waded through the throng.

"What did you think?" Emilia slipped her arm through Jacob's, keeping him close as people pushed their way onto the sidewalk. Large cars with dark windows lined the streets, waiting to whisk the stars away from their adoring fans.

"It was great," Jacob said, trying to maneuver through the crowd. People had lined up, cramming themselves against the ropes that barred them from the stage door.

Emilia laughed as he furrowed his brow in concentration, searching for a path through the human maze in front of them. Jacob saw the gleam in her eye and started to laugh, too. She took his hand and led him toward the street and away from the worst of the crowd, following Iz's bright white hair a few people ahead of them.

It happened in an instant.

Two large men threw open the door of a black SUV and grabbed Emilia, wrenching her hand from his. Before Jacob even knew what was happening, the door of the car slammed shut, dulling Emilia's screams. Jacob leaped toward the door, but the black car sped down the street before he could reach the handle.

"Emilia!" Jacob screamed.

Aunt Iz shouted a spell he didn't recognize, but the car didn't stop. A grate exploded, spewing noxious steam all over the street and allowing the car to disappear around the corner. The crowd panicked, and thousands of people started pushing in every direction, scrambling to find a way out of the sewer haze.

Jacob shoved his way through the panic-stricken crowd, screaming for Emilia, trying to catch a glimpse of the car. But his screams were lost in the sea of chaos, and by the time he fought his way to the street corner, there was no sign of the car or Emilia.

She was gone.

BREATHE

*S*irens echoed in the distance. Someone must have called the police about the grate exploding, but they wouldn't be able to help. Whoever had taken Emilia was beyond the power of the police.

"Emilia! Jacob!" Iz's shouts carried through the crowd. "Jacob," she gasped, grabbing his arm. "Jacob!"

"They're gone." Dazed, Jacob stared up and down Eighth Avenue.

"We have to get home." Iz tried to move Jacob away from the crowd. "Jacob, we have to go home. We can't help her here."

Aunt Iz gripped Jacob's arm and led him through the crowd and into a cab. She was already on the phone with Samuel. Though she said nothing that would arouse the cab driver's suspicion, Jacob knew Samuel would understand exactly what had happened.

Emilia had been taken.

Jacob felt like he would explode sitting in that cab. Every time they stopped at a light, his chest began to constrict. He tried to breathe, but his lungs wouldn't work properly. He dug his nails into the seat, willing the streets to clear so they could get to the house. The black town car in front of them veered suddenly to the left, as though pushed by some invisible giant. The cab driver didn't seem to notice anything strange had happened as he sped into the vacated spot and continued to weave through the midtown traffic.

"Breathe, Jacob." Iz put her hand on his shoulder and stared straight into his eyes, the cell phone still pressed to her ear with the other hand. "*Viridesca*," she muttered, and the light in front of them turned green. "*Sivexi vaiectus.*" The driver did not pause again until they reached the town house.

A flurry of activity had seized the house by the time the cab finally brought Jacob and Iz to the door. Samuel paced the hall, phone pressed to his ear, speaking in a low, urgent tone. There were some other wizards Jacob didn't know by name, but whose faces he recognized from the Council meeting earlier that day. Had it really only been that morning? It seemed like years had passed since he'd sat with Emilia in that sterile, white kitchen.

The small elderly gentleman walked swiftly to Aunt Iz and clasped her hands. "Isadora, we came as soon as we received Samuel's call."

A redheaded witch joined the conversation. "Did you recognize the men?"

"No," Iz said, accepting a hug from the grey-haired black woman who had sat next to her at the meeting. "I've never seen those men, and they weren't bearing any specific signs of allegiance."

"No dragon tattoo?" the grey-haired woman asked.

"No," Jacob said.

Samuel hung up the phone. "I've notified MAGI and called all our friends in the area. MAGI is sweeping the city for unusual magical activity. I've sent people to the Washington Bridge, Lincoln Tunnel, and the rest of the main arteries, but if they leave by water…there's just too much area to cover."

"Have there been any threats? Any indication?" the elderly gentleman asked, his voice quivering.

Iz shook her head. "Nothing that had anything to do with Emilia."

"But after the Council meeting today—" The redheaded witch glanced at Jacob. "Perhaps we should speak in private."

"No," Jacob growled. "Whatever's happening, I want to be involved."

Samuel put his hand on Jacob's shoulder, but Jacob shook it off.

"I don't care what secrets you think you have to keep," Jacob said. "The only thing that matters is finding Emilia, and I can help."

He looked around at the other wizards in the hall. All of them were older than he was. All of them knew more magic than he did. But he loved Emilia, and surely that had to be worth something. If he was locked out of a room while others discussed where she could be, or what might be happening to her, he would go crazy. Jacob turned to Samuel, willing him to understand.

"He's right." Samuel sighed. "We're in no place to reject help from anyone. Especially someone so invested in finding Emilia." He turned to Iz. "We need to call Dexter. I already tried to contact Mr. Wayland, but he didn't answer his phone or my skry."

Iz took out her phone and handed it to Jacob. "Call Dexter. Tell him what happened, and let him know he may come help with the search. Then join us in the dining room. We need to organize. With any luck, we'll receive a ransom demand."

"Would that be a good thing?" Jacob asked.

"It would mean they were interested in my money and not in Emilia's powers," Iz said with a grim twist of her mouth. "That would be a very good thing."

Jacob remembered what Emilia had said when they were in the pantry that morning. Humans locking wizards up. Jacob pictured Emilia in a white room. Trapped. Experimented on.

Emilia's worst nightmare.

A sour taste flooded his mouth.

Aunt Iz led the others into the dining room, leaving Jacob staring at the cell phone in his hand.

He found the number in the phone and called. Jacob paced the hall as Dexter's phone rang.

Ten seconds passed. Jacob wanted Dexter to answer so he could get this horrible conversation over with.

Twenty seconds.

How could he tell someone he hated the girl they both loved was in terrible danger, and that he'd been there but failed to protect her?

The ringing stopped, and Dexter's voice spoke. *You have reached the phone of Dexter Wayland. If you would like me to return your call, please leave a message at the tone. If you do not leave a message, your call will not be returned.*

"Dexter, it's Jacob. Something's happened"—he paused, trying to find the words—"Emilia's been taken. You should be here."

And he hung up. There was nothing more to say.

23

MAGI

*H*ours passed. MAGI agents were on their way. Aunt Iz had tried to skry Emilia, but there was no sign of her.

Aunt Iz tried calling and skrying Mr. Wayland again, but he didn't answer. No one had heard from Dexter either.

A shadow of suspicion fell over the house. Council members were supposed to be reachable at all times, especially after such an explosive meeting.

As soon as the MAGI agents arrived, Aunt Iz pulled them into a side room. Jacob made no attempt to eavesdrop, but he was sure she was saying what no one else in the group dared. The Wayland family was missing. Either they had been kidnapped as well, or they were somehow connected to Emilia being taken.

Finally, Aunt Iz brought the MAGI agents back into the dining room. There were two of them, a man and a woman. The woman, who didn't appear to be much older than Jacob, was petite with a rosy face and blond hair. She didn't seem authoritative or imposing at all. But the man looked like exactly what they needed. He was a very tall, dark-skinned man with huge muscles and a shaved head. He looked, frankly...terrifying.

Aunt Iz introduced the newcomers. "These are MAGI Agents Larkin Gardner and Jeremy Stone."

"We've hacked into the New York Police Department's traffic camera system," MAGI Gardner said. "Unfortunately, the video doesn't show her being pulled into the car. But based on timing and the description of the vehicle, we have narrowed down possible license plate numbers and are currently trying to find out if any of those vehicles have left the city. We are also checking the license plate numbers to see if any of the owners have magical connections. Does anyone have any other information?" She scanned each face in the room.

Jacob was about to say something about Dexter when Samuel caught his eye and gave an almost imperceptible shake of his head. The urge to scream that Dexter must be involved somehow boiled in Jacob, but he held his tongue. He wasn't supposed to know what had happened in the Council meeting after his acquittal earlier that afternoon. And if Samuel thought he shouldn't mention his suspicions, he would have to trust him.

It was a horrible night of waiting. Every hour seemed to last an eternity, and every passing second tightened the knot of fear in Jacob's chest. He thought the night would never end. He would be trapped waiting for the rest of time.

As the sun began to rise, there had still been no news. Gardner and Stone had gone back to headquarters. MAGI Gardner said she needed some information from the Spellnet system. Jacob had a feeling she didn't want to ask another agent to search the computers for whatever it was she needed.

Aunt Iz had installed the Council members into guest rooms. But she herself sat on the couch in the living room, staring into the fire. Samuel had left an hour ago with the usual lack of explanation as to where he was going.

Jacob paced in the dining room. He wanted to explode, to break everything in the house, to scream until his lungs ripped out of his body. But destroying the house would only distract the people who were trying to save Emilia. So he paced.

Where was Dexter? As much as he hated Dexter, Dexter did love Emilia. He must have gotten the message by now. Dexter was usually glued to his phone. But if he had gotten the message, why hadn't he come?

There was only one explanation. Dexter must already know where Emilia was. Even if he hadn't been the one who kidnapped her, he must know who had. On the plus side, Dexter would never let any harm come to Emilia. Dexter might be a jerk, but he would protect her. But what Dexter thought best and what Emilia wanted were not necessarily the same thing.

It didn't matter if Dexter loved her. There was no excuse for taking Emilia away from her family.

Sunlight filled the empty streets. New York City felt like a lie. This city did sleep. It was only he and Iz who didn't.

Claire lay curled up like a kitten, her head on Connor's lap, who was slumped and drooling against the arm of the couch. Neither of them had stirred when each of the three Council members were woken by urgent phone calls dragging them away to deal with crises in their own territories.

Ms. Olivia was the first. A fire on a preserve called her away. A human found dead, burned from the inside out, causing the police to ask unfortunate questions, woke the elderly gentleman less than an hour later. The redheaded woman had to leave when the water from the lake next to her home vanished.

All of them gave their apologies as they left, but there was nothing else to be done. Mayhem had broken out in every territory whose leader had sided with Iz at the Council meeting.

How long would it be before something happened in the Gray lands? Was taking Emilia Iz's punishment for speaking out against the Dragons? Jacob wanted to ask Iz, but how could he explain his theory without telling her he and Emilia had heard everything said after he left the meeting? Was taking Emilia enough, or would the Dragons attack again?

Not that it mattered if the Dragons were planning some other horror. They couldn't stop it, so they would just have to wait. Jacob stared out the window, watching the city come back to life.

He didn't have to wait long for an answer. Molly hadn't even managed to chivvy everyone to breakfast when the professor came stumbling out of his study, white as a sheet. He hung onto the living room doorframe for support. Molly rushed over to him, wrapping an arm around his waist to keep him from collapsing.

"I've just heard from Proteus," the professor said. "There's been an attack at the Graylock Preserve. A group of wizards, some with Dragon tattoos, attacked a hermit wizarding settlement. The hermits called the centaurs for help, but by the time they arrived, the settlement had been slaughtered. The centaurs were ambushed. Proteus and a few others managed to escape, but the rest…" The professor sagged farther into Molly's arms.

"Has MAGI been notified?" Aunt Iz's voice trembled.

Molly led the professor to a chair. "Proteus tried to skry, but all the mirrors showed an empty MAGI office. It looked like it had been ransacked."

"Someone broke into MAGI?" Claire asked, looking around as though hoping someone would tell her it wasn't true. "But it's so well protected. If the MAGI are gone, who's going to help the centaurs? Where's Larkin? She can fix it."

No one answered. No one wanted to tell Claire there was no other help. No one mentioned where Larkin might be.

"There's more," Professor Eames said. "The Dragons at the Graylock Preserve…Proteus thought he recognized their leader. It was Mr. Wayland."

Jacob started shaking. The Council was in shambles. MAGI was gone. The Grays were alone. The people in this room were all they had left.

"We have to go," Jacob said. "If Mr. Wayland is there, Emilia could be there, too. We have to go!"

"I'll arrange transport and leave as soon as possible." Samuel turned to leave the room.

"Me, too." Jacob moved to follow Samuel. "I'm going, too."

"Jacob." Samuel shook his head and laid a hand on Jacob's shoulder. "It's too dangerous for you to go." He stifled Jacob's objection. "I'll go, Jacob, and see if there is any sign of Emilia."

"Samuel," Aunt Iz said quietly. "It's too dangerous to go alone."

"I will go, Isadora," the professor said as he struggled to push himself out of his chair.

"No, Joseph." Iz shook her head.

"I'll go with him," Molly said.

Jacob had heard stories about Molly fighting before, but it was hard for him to picture.

"You need to stay with the children," Iz said. "Someone needs to protect them, and I have to go to MAGI. We need to find out what has happened to them. And I need to find Larkin."

"Then let me go!" Jacob marched over to Iz. "I'll stay out of the way. I'll be careful. But I can't just sit here and wait when we might actually have a shot at rescuing Emilia. Please, Aunt Iz. I have to go."

Iz looked deep into Jacob's eyes. He stared back, hoping he could pass whatever test her mind was putting him through.

Seconds slid past. Iz broke eye contact and squared her shoulders. "Claire, hack the Spellnet system and crash it. If MAGI is out of commission, we can't let the Dragons get ahold of that information. Connor, give her whatever assistance she needs. Molly, help the professor inform our friends of the situation. Be careful not to tell them anything that could endanger Emilia if she is being held at the Graylock Preserve. And try to find a reason the Dragons would choose Graylock to attack.

"Samuel, take Jacob. Try to locate Emilia. Do not attack the

Dragons. Get in and out quickly. If you can rescue Emilia without a fight, do it. If not, come back here. I will try to find some trustworthy wizards who may be willing to help." Aunt Iz took Jacob's hands. "Do exactly as Samuel tells you. Stay hidden. You are only going as the lookout, nothing more. I know you want to bring Emilia home, but think of what she would want. She would never forgive herself if anything happened to you. And neither would I."

Jacob wanted to say he would be careful, but he couldn't form the words. Without meeting her eyes, he squeezed her hands and walked away.

The family separated, each of them going to their appointed tasks. Jacob barely had time to change out of his theatre clothes before Samuel had a car waiting for them outside. The driver whisked them away to a tall building at the very tip of Manhattan. They went up an elevator that made Jacob's ears pop and out onto the roof where a helicopter waited for them.

Jacob didn't know how Samuel had arranged it so quickly, but at this point those types of questions seemed irrelevant. The air from the helicopter's whirling blades beat them back as though it were a living creature determined to keep them from sheltering themselves within its bowels. Samuel put his hand on the back of Jacob's head, forcing him to double over. He didn't let the pressure off until Jacob was safely inside. Even after Samuel had slid the door shut behind him, Jacob could still feel the noise of the churning air vibrating in his chest.

The pilot never spoke. He sat stonily silent until they were ready to take off. Did he know he was flying two wizards to rescue a witch who was being held on land that had been taken in a bloody battle between wizards and centaurs?

Without a word, they flew over the New York skyline as it glistened in the early morning light. The helicopter ride would have been terrifying even if Jacob weren't going into a deadly situation trying to figure out if the girl he loved was still alive. And despite what Aunt Iz wanted, he had no intention of leaving without Emilia.

24

FLESH AND BLOOD

*E*milia was spinning. Her eyes too heavy to open. She felt buried in sand.

Something was very wrong. Her head felt sloshy, and her skin felt dead, as though every inch of her were wrapped in rubber.

But her wrists…there was something strange. She tried to lift her hand to brush the hair away from her face, but her arm was too heavy to move. She breathed deeply and tried to assess her body.

She was sore. Both arms hurt. But why? Why would her arms hurt? It felt like a vice had squeezed them. Or someone had grabbed them.

Men. Big men had grabbed both her arms hard. Very hard. They'd pulled her.

But why?

She took a breath and tried to think. Big men had pulled her into a car.

She wrenched her eyes open, panic bringing her back to her senses. Everything still spun, but she forced herself to sit up.

There were iron cuffs on both of her wrists. They looked like manacles, but there was no chain between them. An inscription in a language Emilia had never seen before had been carved into the cuffs. She tried to focus, to figure out what the writing said, but everything seemed so foggy. It wasn't English. It wasn't Latin. It wasn't even real letters. It looked like runes, but not any she had ever seen. Whatever the cuffs were for, she didn't want to wear them. She tried to pry them off but couldn't find a closure, and they were too tight to slip over her hands.

"*Prolaxio,*" she said, trying to make to cuffs large enough to slip off, but nothing happened. "*Prolaxio,*" she said again, focusing more this time, but still nothing. There wasn't even the tingle that usually came when she did a spell. "*Prolaxio. Prolaxio.*" More and more panic crept into her voice. "*Prolaxio!*"

Her powers were gone. The bracelets had bound her magic. She was as helpless as a human.

Emilia jerked her gaze up. Her prison wasn't what she'd expected. This wasn't a cell or a white padded room. There were no bars or two-way mirrors. The windowless walls were roughly hewn stone. Other than that, it looked like a bedroom. She sat on a bed with an old-fashioned iron frame. A bookcase lined one wall. Clothes had been laid out on an armchair beside the bookcase, with food on the table next to it.

If her powers had been bound, she must have been captured by wizards. A momentary relief flooded her. Wizards wouldn't perform tests on her. Wizards wouldn't cage her up like an animal for experiments.

Her heart raced as fear rushed through her veins.

The Dragons.

"Help!" she screamed, struggling to push herself off the bed. "Somebody help me!"

She stumbled to the wall and tried to bang on it with her fists, but her hands glanced harmlessly away. Again and again, she threw her fists at the wall. A scream of frustration and panic tore from her throat. No matter how hard she swung, she couldn't reach the stone. She *was* in a padded room. It was just padded with magic.

She searched frantically for an exit, but the only door in the room led to the bathroom.

Emilia was trapped.

She went back to the bed and sat down to wait. Someone had gone to the trouble of making her this prison. They clearly wanted her alive...for now. She could only wait for them to turn up. She ignored her hunger. Never touch food from a magical source you don't trust. Every young wizard knew that. She listened to her stomach growl and stared at the blank wall opposite her bed.

Minutes ticked by, but Emilia didn't move. Tears burned in the corners of her eyes.

Jacob. She had been with Jacob. Did they catch him, too?

Emilia jumped to her feet as a horrible scraping sound echoed through the room. A door appeared in the far wall and crept slowly open. She thought about hiding, then pushed her shoulders back, deciding to meet whoever was coming head on. They already knew she was there anyway.

As soon as the door opened completely, a man stepped through, smiling. Tall and handsome with dark curly hair and tanned skin, he couldn't have been even forty, but he had an air of authority about him. He wore an old-fashioned, black military jacket with a red and gold dragon emblazoned across the front.

"Emilia, I heard you were finally awake," the man said as the door swung slowly shut behind him. "I am so pleased to finally meet you." He scrutinized Emilia from her bare feet to the top of her disheveled head, as though searching for something.

"Where am I?" Emilia asked.

"You are at the Graylock Preserve, which is now the headquarters of the Dragons," the man answered.

Emilia had assumed it was the Dragons who'd kidnapped her, but the man's confirmation only made her more nervous. She dug her nails into her palms, trying to keep the tears from forming in her eyes. "What do the Dragons want with me?"

"Nothing." The man spread his hands. "The Dragons have no interest in you, even though you were Isadora Gray's ward. And Isadora does tend to cause trouble." He shook his head. "I am afraid it is I who has an interest in you, Emilia, and it was I who ordered my men to bring you here."

Emilia grabbed the lamp from the nightstand, ready to defend herself. But the man only laughed.

"Please, Emilia, do not upset yourself. I would never dream of harming you in any way. In fact, I was very displeased to find how bruised you were from my men rescuing you. I assure you they have been punished. I will not allow anyone here to hurt you. You are under my protection, and as it is only by my pleasure the Dragons live, my protection is infallible."

"Then why did you bring me here?" Emilia asked, not relaxing her grip on the lamp.

"Please don't be afraid. I know taking you like that must have been quite a shock, but I promise no harm will come to you here. I regret the anxiety I must have caused you, but it was the only way. Isadora would never have let me see you otherwise."

"Why would you want to see me?" Emilia asked.

"Because I am your father," the man answered simply.

The lamp slipped in her hands. "You're lying," she said through gritted teeth, retightening her grip. "You are not my father."

"How could you possibly know? You've never met your father. Well, here I am!" The man laughed and held out his hand. "My followers call me the Pendragon, but my name is Emile LeFay. I must say I am so very pleased your mother named you after me."

He waited for Emilia to take his hand, but she backed away as far as she could, leaning into the wall behind her.

"I am sorry to only be meeting you now. Your mother never told me." The Pendragon lowered his hand, looking unsure of himself for the first time. "She never told me she was expecting you. But I knew as soon as I saw a picture of you with that necklace. You look so much like her, and I gave that necklace to your mother when she came to this very preserve with me many years ago. You are my child, Emilia. There is absolutely no doubt about that. *Darthera undolfa ebghodt.*"

A bright glow surrounded the Pendragon, forming red tendrils that seemed to taste the air around him. Slowly, the light reached for Emilia, wrapping around her arms and neck. "You see, my child, blood knows blood."

Emilia felt the world shift. The spell had pulled all the air from the room. The lamp slipped from her hands, and the *crash* as it hit the floor echoed as though from far away.

The Pendragon rushed over to Emilia and tried to lead her away from the broken glass to sit at the table. Emilia shook him off.

"No! Aunt Iz is my family. I don't know you." She stepped away from him. Glass sliced painfully into her foot. The Pendragon caught her arm and lifted her effortlessly over to the chair. Before she could say anything, he had crouched on the floor to pull the glass from her foot.

"Isadora Gray is not your family. I am sorry I was not able to raise you, but you are my child." He muttered a healing spell, and Emilia winced at the sting of her skin knitting back together.

"You kidnapped me." Emilia yanked her foot away from him.

"I took my daughter back. I don't think there is anything wrong with that."

"I'm not your daughter."

He stared into Emilia's eyes. "I know it will take you some time to trust me, but I want to get to know you. Is that so wrong?"

"It's wrong to take a person prisoner, especially when you bring them to the base for a group of murderers."

"You are not a prisoner. You are my guest. My hope, Emilia, is to convince you of how wrong you are about me. About all of us. I am the leader of the Dragons, but we are not murderers. We are freedom fighters determined to create a better world. Just imagine, Emilia." The Pendragon sat opposite her, a manic gleam in his eyes. "A new world with no more war or hunger or pollution. The humans need to be governed. They have made a mess of this world, but I will fix it. I will create a new world in which magic reigns. Where the laws I make will be obeyed. And I will do it with my daughter at my side."

"I am not your daughter," Emilia said again, trying not to show fear as she glared into the Pendragon's eyes.

Grey eyes that looked so much like her own.

25

GRAYLOCK

*T*he helicopter landed in a clearing ten miles away from the preserve. The only time the pilot spoke was when he shouted, "You're on your own to get back," right before he took off.

A black jeep waited for them near a dirt road, which was the only break in the line of trees. Samuel had planned well. The jeep was fueled, and keys waited for them in the ignition.

They climbed in quickly, and Samuel drove down the bumpy road at top speed. "We can't approach from any of the main roads. The Dragons will be watching those. The best we can do is drive most of the way up the mountain on the far side. There are enough back roads to get us there. Once we get near the top, we leave the car and hike two miles down to the opening of the hermit's cave systems, which, according to our sources, is where the Dragons should be." Samuel took a sharp left turn, and Jacob banged his head into the window. "We'll get as close as we can to the entrance without running into any shield spells they might have working for them. Then, we watch."

Samuel braked suddenly, and Jacob grunted as his seatbelt pulled him painfully back. Samuel turned to him. "I know how badly you want her back. I've known Emilia her whole life. I want to get her back, too, but getting captured or killed won't help her. It will only leave fewer people on the outside trying to save her. Got it?" After Jacob nodded, Samuel continued. "If I choose to go in, you have to stay behind. It's the only way Iz can stay informed, and you can contact her if we need help. Do you understand?"

"Yes," Jacob said, comforted that Samuel was willing to go in after Emilia, even if it wasn't what Iz had instructed. It made Jacob feel less guilty about disobeying Iz.

"We will get her back, Jacob." Samuel grabbed Jacob's shoulder before turning back to the road and continuing his race through the woods.

They met no one on their ride up Mount Graylock. But Jacob could feel something dark surrounding the mountain. The air felt alive with energy, an energy intent on malice.

Samuel swung the jeep off the road and through a clump of brush before stopping and hopping out. He pulled two packs and his staff from the back of the jeep. "We might be here awhile." He strapped his pack on then handed Jacob a pocket mirror.

The mirror was small and distinctly feminine. Jacob ran his thumb over the red enamel roses covering the back.

"The professor taught you how to skry?"

Jacob nodded.

"Good. If we get separated, contact me immediately." Without waiting for a response, Samuel walked to the brush he had flattened with the jeep. He planted the end of his staff on the ground, and the stems and branches snapped back to attention. No one would be able to spot the jeep now. Avoiding the road, Samuel started hiking up the mountain.

"Stay close to me, and keep quiet," Samuel said in a hushed tone. "We need to go unnoticed, so we can't use magic to move. They could sense a spell that big."

Jacob struggled to keep up. He had never done any hiking,

and though he was athletic, it was hard for him to find his footing. He did all right climbing to the top of the mountain. It was down that was difficult. There didn't seem to be a solid place to step. Whenever he slid or broke a branch, Samuel narrowed his eyes reproachfully but said nothing. They couldn't afford to make noise.

The heat of the day had begun to break through the trees when Samuel veered left, away from their former course. He stopped behind a tree and waited for Jacob to catch up.

"The entrance to the caverns should be just under that rise," Samuel whispered, pointing to what seemed like no more than a mound of rocks carelessly piled onto a misplaced hill. "But I haven't seen any guards yet. We're going to go in low and slow." Samuel pointed to a fallen tree a hundred yards downhill from them. "We should be able to see the entrance from there."

Samuel got down on his stomach and crawled forward. Jacob followed, the downed branches tearing at his forearms and stomach. Samuel stopped every few feet to listen. But there was only silence. Finally, they reached the tree, and both of them peered carefully over its vast trunk.

Samuel's sources had been right. They had indeed found the Dragons.

A man stood at either side of the cave's entrance, dressed in identical black uniforms with blood red dragons emblazoned across their chests. Both guards had shaved heads, which allowed full view of the dragon tattoo etched into each man's skin, beginning at their left ears and winding down their necks. In front of the entrance to the cave, seven witches and wizards sat holding hands. Their mouths moved as one, chanting a spell Jacob couldn't hear. There were only nine guards. Nine against two weren't horrible odds.

"We could go in," he whispered to Samuel, "if we take them by surprise. We have cover. They don't."

"Wait," Samuel said. "*Admeo amisculum.*" Samuel kept his eyes closed.

Jacob scanned from the green tops of the trees to the dead and decaying leaves on the ground, trying to see what effect Samuel's spell might have had.

After a few moments, there was a faint scurrying in the bushes. A small mouse appeared and ran straight into Samuel's waiting hands. "I am sorry, my friend," he said, petting the mouse. "Thank you." He placed the mouse on the ground, and it hurried off toward the cave entrance.

Jacob tracked the mouse by the telltale shaking of the fallen leaves. The mouse was getting close to the cave entrance. It was only a hundred feet away when a bright flash lit the sky as a brilliantly glowing dome appeared around the entrance to the cave. A bolt of lightning ran down the side of the dome. A *crack* of energy and a horrid *squeal* from the mouse rent the silence as the bolt struck the ground.

A moment later, the dome had disappeared, and the sky returned to a perfect pale blue. Jacob rubbed his eyes, trying to rid them of the spots the sudden flash had caused.

By the time he could see clearly, the guards were already moving cautiously forward to where the lighting had hit. One guard held out his wand and the other his right fist, where a gold ring glinted in the sunlight. They seemed satisfied the field mouse had been the only intruder. The men laughed at the poor dead creature, but still, Jacob could hear nothing. As the men returned to their posts, the stench of burning flesh reached Jacob's nostrils, stinging them with the scent of death.

"The circle is making a shield, and a good one at that," Samuel whispered as they crouched behind the tree.

"They're blocking noise, too?"

"Yep, but we don't know if it's only a one-way block. They may still be able to hear us. Whoever is running this place has it very well guarded. As long as that circle is intact, no one can get in."

"Can we send a spell in to distract the people in the circle?" Jacob asked.

"It's not worth the risk. With a shield like that, it could take several tries to see if any spell could break through. And as soon as one spell failed, we would have given away our position."

Samuel drew a half circle with his staff, enclosing them with the downed tree. Then he chanted slowly under his breath. Jacob picked out a few words here and there, but it was definitely not a spell the professor had covered.

"It's a rough chameleon spell," Samuel said when he finished his chant almost a minute later. "We can't risk anything stronger. They can't see or hear us as long as we stay within the line. But if they try to come through..." Samuel shrugged.

"No deadly lightning. Got it." Jacob peered over the tree. "So what do we do now?"

"We wait for someone to enter or exit the shield. That will show us how they get through and give us a better idea of what sort of spell it is."

They took turns watching all day and through the night. The packs had food, water, and blankets, but it was still a long, cold night on the mountain. Jacob had forgotten he hadn't slept in more than a day. When it was Samuel's turn to watch, his body took over, forcing him into sleep even though his anxious mind refused to relax.

Daybreak brought the changing of the guards outside the cave. Seven people came to replace the spell casters, but the seated circle didn't stop chanting. The replacements stepped over their joined hands and formed their own circle in the center. As soon as they were all settled, the new circle joined hands and began to chant.

The new dome formed exactly where Jacob had seen the old one flash. As its walls blossomed downward, it shimmered in the pink sunlight of dawn and was, for a moment, almost beautiful. As soon as the new dome was complete, the outer circle stood up stiffly and stumbled their way into the cave, some helping one another, others chatting tiredly.

"There won't be a chance to get through at a shift change," Samuel said. "They have that covered."

Hours passed, and nothing happened outside the cave. Jacob's foot twitched to an awkward rhythm and his nails dug pits into the dirt. The urge to leap out of hiding and run for the cave entrance grew every minute.

Emilia could be under this hill. Somewhere under these rocks, she could be trapped, scared, or hurt. What if someone were hurting her right now? Anger and panic rose in his chest. He wanted to run, to scream, to attack. Jacob had to force himself to breathe. If he let his magic get out of control now, they could very easily be found.

The sun had climbed high in the sky when something finally happened. Three men emerged from the cave, all of them big, burly, and bald. Two of the men talked to the guards, while the third stood away from the conversation.

The third man looked familiar. An angry red streak broke through his dragon tattoo.

Jacob pointed him out to Samuel. "It's the man from the plane. His ears. Emilia melted his earphones into his ears."

"That's my girl." Samuel chuckled. "He should've gotten worse, if you ask me."

The men moved toward the shield. Samuel and Jacob both tensed, waiting for the shield to drop. Even if Jacob and Samuel weren't going to try to get to the cave, hearing a part of the incantation might give them an idea of how to break through it. But the chanting never stopped. The men passed straight through the shield, which shimmered slightly but didn't strike them down.

"I bet that brat was surprised. He didn't expect to have her locked up. Thought he would get her all to himself," one of the men said, laughing as the sun gleamed off of his closely shaven head.

"I guess his daddy didn't do enough to buy him his girlfriend. Money doesn't matter much to the Pendragon, does it?" the second man answered.

Both guffawed loudly. The man from the plane put his hands to the side, clearly asking what the other two were laughing about.

"Money!" The first man shouted. "The Pendragon doesn't need the Waylands' damn money!"

The airplane man still shook his head.

"Forget it," the second man said. "That pretty little thing had better be grateful Laurent here hasn't gotten his hands on her yet. Won't be so pretty after that." He pantomimed to the airplane man what he thought he should do to Emilia. The airplane man laughed, and the Dragons walked down the hill, the first two talking carelessly as they went.

Samuel grabbed Jacob's shoulder and forced him back down. Jacob hadn't even noticed he had stood, ready to fight the men. He put his head in his hands, pulling his hair, desperately trying to put his thoughts into some workable order.

Emilia was here. They knew that now. Someone called the Pendragon had her. She was locked up somewhere under the mountain. Bile rose into Jacob's throat.

Dexter was here. His father was working with this Pendragon, and they had helped to bring Emilia here. Laurent wanted to hurt Emilia, and it sounded like he might soon be given the chance.

26

FIRST BLOOD

*S*amuel turned Jacob around to face him, pulling him out of his horrible thoughts. "We have to tell Iz what we know," Samuel said. "If Emilia really is in there, we need to get her out as soon as possible. We also need to call off the search for the Waylands. It's a waste of resources now that we know where they are."

Jacob expressed his opinion of the Waylands with a string of choice expletives.

"I agree," Samuel said. "First, we get Emilia out, and then we get the Wayland scum."

"How did they get out of the barrier?" Jacob studied the cave entrance, more determined than ever to get in.

"I think it might be the dragon tattoos." Samuel pointed at the guards. "Those two have tattoos, and so did the three who left. But none of the chanters do. If I were in charge, I'd make sure the only people who could get through the shield were the people I expected to charge through it to protect the compound from danger. I think the tattoo is like a password."

Jacob nodded, the beginnings of a plan forming is his mind.

"I can't skry Iz from inside the shield," Samuel said. "I'm going up the hill and out of sight. I should be back within a half hour. Stay here and watch the entrance. See what else you can learn."

Jacob nodded, and Samuel silently disappeared up the mountain. Jacob studied the circle casting the invisible shield, waiting for the three men to return. But there was no movement at all. The chanters continued their muted spell, and the guards stood like statues at the entrance to the cave. There weren't even any birds flying overhead. Silence filled the forest.

More than an hour later, Samuel still had not returned. Jacob tried to convince himself Samuel was busy planning a rescue mission with Iz. Maybe Iz had found some MAGI agents and was sending them here. Then Samuel would have to wait for them.

But after another silent hour, Jacob's gnawing dread had grown into an absolute certainty that something had gone wrong.

He pulled out the little red mirror. He would have to leave the shield to contact Samuel. But would he be able to get back into it? *Lingua Venificium* hadn't mentioned reentry into someone else's spell. He would have to risk it.

Jacob slid on his pack and quietly crawled out of the shield. There was a cluster of trees up ahead. If he could make it there, he could stand up and move more quickly. He did just as Samuel had done, stopping to check for sounds every few feet, but he heard nothing.

Finally, he reached the trees and was hidden from the entrance. He stood up and crept noiselessly through the woods. He traveled sideways across the face of the mountain, hoping that even if someone had found Samuel's trail, he would be too far away to be noticed on the same search.

Jacob scanned the area, satisfied no one else would be able to hear him. "*Volavertus* Samuel," he whispered into the red mirror. The mirror glowed brightly in his hand. He waited for Samuel to accept his skry. But instead of Samuel's image appearing, the glow of his mirror slowly dulled, leaving only the reflection of the sky peering through the branches above him.

Wherever Samuel was, he was unable to talk. Jacob had just decided to try contacting Iz himself when the sharp *crack* of a branch breaking sounded behind him. He ducked behind a tree and cautiously peered around the side.

It was the airplane man, but this time he traveled alone. He mumbled to himself, but it was much louder than most people mumble. He seemed unsure if he was actually making noise. "Scratch her face off, and then maybe I'll see what the rest of her sweet little body has to offer." The man cackled to himself. "The Pendragon owes me that much. I was willing to die. Least he can do is give me that damn girl."

Jacob's blood boiled. All thoughts of magic forgotten, he reached down and grabbed a large stick. Not even bothering to be quiet, he ran up behind the man and hit him hard on the head. The airplane man never heard him coming.

Jacob gaped at the unconscious, bleeding man. Blood shone on the end of his stick.

He dropped it, his hands shaking. He had never hurt someone on purpose before. The man on the ground was still breathing, but Jacob had definitely done some damage. His mind raced, flitting between a dozen half-formed plans.

He didn't care what Iz wanted anymore. He didn't care what happened to himself. From what the man currently lying unconscious at Jacob's feet in a growing pool of blood had said, Emilia was going to be given to one of these thugs.

"*Strigo motus.*" Now the man couldn't wake up and resist.

Even though Jacob was strong from years of hard work, he struggled to heave the unconscious man onto his shoulders. The man's warm blood dripped onto Jacob's neck. Jacob's legs shook as he started slowly up the mountain, careful to stay out of sight.

The shield reached to the top of the rock mound above the cave, and that was where Jacob approached, behind the rocks so no one could see. He slowed when he neared the shield and shifted his passenger onto his back like a cape. Making sure the man's shoulders covered his head, he stepped into the barrier.

A cool breeze tickled Jacob's bare skin, but no bolt came from above to strike him down. He had made it through the shield. He was inside the camp. Now he needed to get inside the cave. The chanting was audible now, and even in the bright sunlight, the eerie sound sent a shiver down Jacob's spine.

He slid the airplane man off his back and laid him quietly in the leaves, resisting the urge to land a sharp kick in his ribs. Jacob carefully climbed the rocks in front of him, hoping to see the cave entrance from above. From his perch, he saw the circle chanting and heard them clearly, but it wasn't a spell he recognized. The guards were hidden from view by the outcropping of rocks under his feet.

Jacob cursed to himself. He could either come at the guards head on or jump down from the top of the cave entrance and hope to surprise them. Neither option seemed to hold much hope for success.

He slid down the rocks and tried to think. There had to be a way to get into the cave. He must have learned some spell that could help him.

Jacob reviewed each spell he knew. He went through them alphabetically, just as he would have if he had been studying for a school exam, but it was too hard to concentrate. He would never find the right spell. All the words from the chant kept mixing with the spells in his mind. He should have thought on the other side of the shield when he had silence.

Then Jacob found the answer. He needed to figure out which chant they were using to create the shield charm. He could memorize the chant, use the airplane man to get back out of the shield, skry Iz, and ask for backup. After that, they would be able to break through the shield, rescue Emilia, and find Samuel.

Crawling carefully, Jacob climbed back up the rocks, listening for the exact enunciation of the spell. He closed his eyes, focusing on the chant until he could repeat it with the circle. He smiled, confident he could remember the wording exactly.

He turned to climb back down the rocks, and everything went black.

27

TRAPPED IN STONE

*J*t was dark and cold. Jacob was curled up on the floor. He tried to sit up but smacked his head painfully on the ceiling. He reached above his head and met a solid stone wall. He tried to stretch out his legs, but after a few inches they hit stone as well. He kicked down with his feet, but the wall wouldn't move.

Jacob's heart raced, his pulse thudding in his ears. He was trapped in a stone box. He had never been claustrophobic, but this was too much. Jacob groped around for his wand, hoping against hope he might find it trapped with him.

It wasn't.

His breath came in quick gasps. He was trapped and helpless.

Jacob tried to calm his breathing, wanting to preserve his precious and dwindling supply of air. How had he gotten here?

He'd been outside. It was bright, and there was lots of air—

No, Jacob warned himself, *don't focus on the air.*

He had memorized the chant, he was going to leave the shield, and then…maybe he fell into this hole.

You can't fall into a place that has a solid stone ceiling.

He must have been ambushed. He'd been so focused on the chant he hadn't kept proper watch. He hadn't gotten Iz the information, Samuel didn't know where he was, and Emilia was still in trouble.

He needed to get out of this tomb. No. Box, it was only a box. Jacob couldn't let himself think the word *tomb*.

Jacob ran his fingers along the edges of his prison, hoping to find a way to pry the box open. He felt his way blindly in the dark, reaching as far as he could toward his feet, but he didn't have enough room to switch where his shoulders and hips were. He started to work his way back up—maybe he had missed something—when the top of the box moved.

Jacob pushed his fingers harder into a corner, trying desperately to pry the lid off his stone coffin, but the crack shifted away from him. The box was expanding. The ceiling was getting higher. Jacob pushed himself onto his knees and continued searching the walls. If he had made his prison expand, maybe he could find a way out, too.

The box was the size of a small room now and emitted a horrible noise as it grew. The stone screamed as its surfaces raked across each other. It sounded like a hundred nails scraping across shrieking blackboards. Jacob resisted the urge to cover his ears, which felt as though they might explode.

The scraping finally stopped, and the walls ceased their growth. A torch flared to life inches in front of his face. He tried to blink the blinding spots out of his eyes. The scraping started again, but this time it was only coming from the wall behind him. Jacob turned and faced the opening door.

A woman entered the room. She smiled, and just from that usually friendly facial expression Jacob knew she was definitely not the sort of person he wanted to be trapped in this room with. The woman was tall with flowing, white-blond hair. Dressed in tight black pants, with spike-heeled boots, and a tight leather top with a red dragon embossed across her chest, for a moment, Jacob thought he had been captured by Catwoman.

"Hello, Jacob," the woman said as she pressed the door closed behind her. "You have been a very bad boy, sneaking into our camp. Although"—the woman smiled again—"I am very impressed at how you did it. Poor Laurent will be severely punished, which means more fun for me. Though I do hate to play with broken toys."

"Who are you?" Jacob asked, somewhat pleased that, if he was going to be killed, at least the airplane man was going down, too. Emilia would not be a treat for him.

"Domina." She held out her hand as though expecting Jacob to kiss it. When he didn't, she continued. "I am the Pendragon's special helper, among other things. And the Pendragon is very pleased you are here. In fact, he would have much preferred you to walk up to the shield and ask to be let in. Then, you would have been greeted as an honored guest. But with all of your sneaking around, the Pendragon has decided you can't be trusted. Which means you're all mine." She reached out and caressed Jacob's cheek. She slid her ice cold fingers down his neck and dug her black nails into his chest.

Jacob tried to ignore the pain. "Who is this Pendragon?"

"The Pendragon is your lord and master. He controls all that happens here, and soon, very soon, he will control everything. *Subnicio.*"

Something hit Jacob hard in the back of the knees, sending him to the ground. "Where's Emilia?" He stood, unwilling to kneel at this woman's feet, suddenly afraid she might do worse to Emilia than the doomed airplane man.

Domina raised her eyebrows and grinned. "If you knew what I could do to you, you wouldn't be so worried about Emilia. After all, the Pendragon would never let anyone hurt his precious little baby girl. Especially after he went to all the trouble of having her kidnapped. That was quite a bother."

"What? The leader of the Dragons is pretending Emilia is his daughter?"

"Not pretending, my pet," Domina said, almost purring at Jacob's shock.

"That's not true," Jacob spluttered. "That's impossible."

"Give me one good reason."

Jacob wracked his brain, rushing through everything Emilia had told him about her past. But he couldn't think of any real reason it couldn't be true. Emilia had never known anything about her father or mother. How could he prove who her father wasn't?

"Emilia is going to be the princess when the new world order is complete. Sitting at the left hand of her beloved daddy. The right hand is all mine. The real question is will you be alive to hear the wonderful tales of the Pendragon's ascension? I do tell very good stories." Domina pulled a wand from her waistband. "*Tendicanis.*" She gave a lazy flick of her wand.

Jacob flew through the air. His back slammed into the wall behind him, knocking the breath from his body, but instead of falling to the ground, he remained pinned, his arms splayed at his sides. Pressure like gravity itself held Jacob to the wall. He couldn't turn his head or even flex a finger. He tried fruitlessly to free himself, struggling against his invisible bonds as Domina slunk forward.

Domina blew a long, slow breath on her wand. The tip glowed a bright red, and the air around it crackled. She gazed at the tip of her wand lovingly, like it was a work of art she had created. Then she moved it toward Jacob's face. Even with the wand still more than a foot away, it radiated an intense heat. She trailed her wand carefully through the air, as though deciding which part of his face she wanted to brand.

Jacob wanted more than anything to pull away from the heat and inevitable pain.

Domina smiled as she put her cheek on his, her breath

caressing his neck as she whispered, "You will never see the outside of this room again. It is either your prison or your tomb. Do as I say, and you may live long enough to call this place home."

For a moment, pain seared Jacob's cheek, and then he knew no more.

28

SCREAMS IN THE DARK

*E*milia sat with her legs curled beneath her in the armchair, reading a book entitled *The Master Race*. All of the books on her shelf were like that. Every one of them expounded upon the superiority of Magickind.

Every gardener knows the lives of the weeds must be sacrificed to ensure the growth of the flower. Evolution cries for a rise of Magickind. Perpetuating the lives of the weak and non-magical is a detrimental practice that must cease.

Cleansing the world. Genocide. The writings made Emilia sick. But she had been locked in that room for God only knew how long, and at least hating the books gave her something to do.

The door began to scrape open and Emilia assumed it was someone bringing her food again. It should be dinner next. That was the only way she knew what time of day it was. Eggs in the morning, sandwich in the afternoon, and a hot meal for dinner.

But the person who came through the door was not carrying a tray.

"Dexter." Emilia leaped to her feet and ran toward the door as it began to scrape shut behind him. "Don't let it close," she cried, but he caught her around the waist and held her back as the door joined seamlessly with the solid wall. "Dex, we have to get out of here!"

"Em, you're all right." Dexter pulled her against his chest and buried his face in her hair.

Emilia tried to push him away so he could see how dire their situation was. But instead, he kissed her. Not a panicked kiss, but a kiss of relief. A wonderfully, blissfully normal kiss. Dexter was warm and there, and so familiar. Emilia sagged into his arms, letting his kiss wash away all her worry and fear if only for a moment.

Finally, she pulled away. "Dexter, we're locked in, and they bound my magic. But maybe you can still get us through the door. Or get these cuffs off so we can both fight."

Dexter just stared.

"We have to get out of here. I don't know how much time we have until someone figures out you've come for me." Emilia took his hand and pulled him toward the wall. She ran her hands over where the door had been, but her fingers slid over the magical barrier that would not let her reach the stone.

"No, Em," Dexter said, pulling her hands from the wall, "you can't leave."

Emilia stared at Dexter's calm, almost relieved, face, not understanding what he could possibly mean.

"I'm sorry, but you have to stay in here."

Emilia yanked her hands away from his.

"I know you're angry right now, and I'm sure I would be, too."

Backing away, she met the wall and crept sideways, putting distance between herself and this fake Dexter. Imposter Dexter. Dexter, the real Dexter, her boyfriend, would never want to keep her locked up.

"All right." Dexter raised his hands and stayed very still. "Look, I won't touch you, but please listen to me. You have to stay in this room. We might be attacked—"

"We?" Emilia spat at him.

"Fine, the Dragons. The Dragons could be attacked at any time, and the safest place for you is right here in this room."

"The safest place for me is at home with my family. Not locked up underground."

"Emilia, your family is here. I'm here. Your father is here." Dexter took a step forward.

"You knew? You knew, and you didn't tell me?" Emilia grabbed the first book within reach and threw it at Dexter's head.

The corner hit him hard in the mouth. He wiped away the blood with his thumb. "I deserved that."

"You deserve a hell of a lot worse."

"For protecting you? There is a war coming. And who knows how big it's going to be? The Pendragon is right. Things have to change in order for us to survive. The Dragons are more powerful than we ever thought. I love you, Em. Your father loves you. Is it so terrible for us to want you to be on the winning side of this mess? And trust me, we will win."

"At what cost?" Emilia snatched another, bigger book off the shelf. "How much blood are you willing to spill in order to win? And don't you dare tell me that freak LeFay loves me. One of his men tried to bring down the plane I was on!" Emilia was screaming now. She pitched the second book at Dexter, who swatted it away with his bloody hand. "And you knew, didn't you? You tried to keep me off the plane, but you were perfectly willing to let Iz and Jacob die!"

"I didn't know there was an attack planned," Dexter said, his face paling a shade. "My father only said there was room on the helicopter for you."

Dexter moved forward and reached for Emilia's hand, but she shook him away, disgusted at the very sight of him.

"You have to know, Emilia, I would never hurt you. I would never let anyone hurt you."

"And Aunt Iz and Jacob? Do you think their deaths wouldn't

hurt me? And the hundred other people on the plane? What about them? They don't matter to you, do they, Dexter? You wouldn't mind if they died."

"No! I never said that. I told you I didn't know. I didn't know what the Dragons were planning. I didn't even know the Pendragon was your father until I got here." He took a slow step forward, approaching her with both arms outstretched, as though she were a wounded animal. "All I know is I love you, and together we can figure out what or who is wrong in all this mess."

Emilia shook her head. "Oh, Dex. How can you even question who's wrong?"

"Don't you see? This is our chance. To break free from all the hiding, all the secrets. We could show the world who we are. What we can do," Dexter said, his eyes fierce with determination. "The centaurs and fawns could walk the streets. No more hiding on preserves."

"How?" Emilia asked. "How can you possibly think this could work? Humans will never accept us."

"Then we make them. We attack. We show them who the dominant species is. We take back our land. They can't compete with magic."

"Then you'll kill people. Innocent people. And once their blood is on your hands, they'll come after us with bombs and guns." Emilia's voice rose with her anger. "Dexter, you're starting a war. A real war. And it could be a massacre for Magickind. We're outnumbered."

"But a shield spell can stop bullets, and even bombs."

"What? How do you—"

"The Dragons have done tests. There are bases and plans." Dexter captured Emilia's face in his hands. "This isn't a misplaced rebellion. It's an army ready for war."

"You really don't care then?" Her voice cracked with choked back tears. "You don't care how many humans die?"

"No." Dexter shook his head. "And neither will you once we take our rightful place at the head of this world's society."

"If you really think that, Dexter, you don't know me." She pulled his hands away from her face. "And I certainly don't know you."

"Em…"

"Get out," Emilia whispered. "Get out!"

Dexter fled for the door, which scraped shut right as Emilia's lamp crashed into the stone.

～

*E*milia walked across the dunes. A chill breeze whispered through the night air, but the sand still held the warmth of the day. She paused at the peak of the highest dune, watching the moon play on the waves as they gently lapped up to the shore. A woman stood with her feet in the water. Emilia couldn't see the woman's face, but it was her. It had to be.

She ran toward the woman, wanting more than anything to see her, to speak with her. She had so many questions. She had to reach her. But the sand kept shifting, and try as she might, Emilia could get no closer to the shore.

Emilia searched the dunes for another path to the beautiful woman at the water's edge, but she found none.

She turned back to the woman, ready to call out for help. A wave surged up to the shore dragging the woman under the water and out of sight.

～

"*M*other!" Emilia woke up screaming, her bed drenched with sweat.

"Don't be afraid, my Emilia."

Emilia squinted at the figure sitting at the foot of her bed.

"Did you have a bad dream?" LeFay reached for her, but she pulled away. He smiled grimly and stood up. "It is such a pity I wasn't there when you were a child. If you had been with me, I would have made sure you were never afraid of anything. But alas, we cannot change the past." He sat down at the table, which was laden with a much fancier breakfast than Emilia had been given on the other mornings she had spent locked in the stone room. "Please join me. We must do something to celebrate this special day."

"Special?" Emilia asked, her lips pressed flat as she joined LeFay at the table. "The only thing I want to celebrate is you letting me out of here."

"Not possible. I know you are a very determined and strong-willed young woman, which pleases me immensely. But in this case, Father knows best." LeFay poured them both orange juice. "A toast to the protection of my only child."

Emilia didn't raise her glass.

LeFay put his glass back down and folded his hands under his chin, leaning on the table. "You see, Emilia dear, I have formed such a clever plan. It will ensure you remain safely in the protection of the Dragons. It will solidify the allegiance of a very important family, and it will eventually bring you much joy."

Emilia already didn't like the sound of his plan. Not at all. "What would bring me much joy would be going home." She stood up, no longer hungry enough to stay at a table with him.

"That is not a possibility right now. However, if you sit down and eat with me, we will discuss your being allowed out of this room. I am prepared to offer you free rein of the compound."

The Pendragon's gaze didn't falter as Emilia stared him down. He seemed to be telling the truth.

"All I am asking is to eat a meal with my daughter. After we eat, we will discuss how best to maintain your security while giving you a chance to see more of your father's home."

Emilia sat down grudgingly. Getting out of the room would get her one step closer to escaping and getting home.

LeFay raised his glass to toast Emilia again. "To my growing family."

Emilia toasted and took a sip. She was unconscious before her glass shattered on the floor.

29

WORSE THAN PAIN

*J*acob trembled. He hadn't had anything to eat or drink since he had been captured. His right cheek throbbed from Domina's burn.

The room had shrunk to an even smaller size than his original box when Domina left. Now, it was too short for him to straighten his back. Every muscle in his body had seized up and beat its protest with every breath he drew. He wanted to sleep, to fade from consciousness until he didn't hurt anymore.

He had heard someone screaming before. He hadn't recognized the voice, but pain could easily contort a person beyond recognition. At least it wasn't Emilia. Her father wouldn't allow her to be tortured.

The darkness had gone quiet now. The screaming had stopped, maybe ten minutes before, perhaps a few hours. If only his stomach were full, he could sleep.

Food and water would come soon. Dehydrating to death would be too quick and quiet for Domina. She would want to play with him more before he died.

So he waited, thinking of Emilia. Hoping she would find a way out without his help. He had tried to form an escape plan, but since he didn't know where he was, how many guards there might be, or if anyone was trying to rescue him, hoping for an opportunity was really all he could do.

He had almost slipped into a fitful sleep when a horrible scraping sound pierced his brain. The room rumbled as the walls expanded.

Jacob pushed himself to his knees and tried to straighten his spine, biting his cheeks to keep himself from screaming in pain. He crawled to the wall and forced himself up, refusing to be found hunched in a ball in his cell, defeated.

A torch burst into flames. Jacob focused on the wall opposite the torch, trying to get his eyes to adjust to the first light he'd seen since Domina had left.

A chink of light formed on the wall to his left as Domina opened the stone door and entered his cell. She tossed a jar to Jacob. His arms were so stiff and heavy he barely caught it.

"Broth." Domina smiled as she closed the door behind her. "We need to keep your strength up."

Jacob opened the jar and sniffed carefully before taking a small sip. It was cold, but better than nothing.

Domina leaned casually against the wall, smiling at him like a lioness that had cornered her prey.

Then Jacob noticed her belt. His wand stuck out beneath the leather. She was so arrogant she had brought his wand into his cell, assuming he could never take it from her, or perhaps hoping he would try.

Domina caught Jacob staring at the wand, and her smile broadened. "I think it matches my outfit. Don't you? I like to collect things. Talismans from my..." She searched for the words for a moment, twisting a ring inscribed with a tiny bird she wore on her left hand. "Expired playmates. I know you're still alive, but since you won't be needing it any longer, I thought you wouldn't mind if I started to play with it a bit early."

The fury in Jacob's stomach threatened to expel his broth.

"Now, little Jakey-poo," Domina crooned, "don't be angry with me." She scooped her finger through the air as though scooping frosting off a cake.

Jacob watched in horror as the air around her finger started to glow, forming a purple, crackling ball of light. He didn't have time to breathe before she threw the ball hard into his right shoulder. Jacob gasped when his head cracked into the wall behind him. The jar slid from his hand and shattered, but he couldn't see anything through the bright spots of light dancing before his eyes.

Domina laughed. A high, gleeful, girlish laugh, more suited to a child chasing butterflies than a woman bent on torture.

Jacob pushed away from the wall, taking deep breaths to steady himself. But before the room had stopped spinning, Domina hurled another crackling ball at his left knee, which buckled beneath him. He tried to catch himself but was too weak from the lack of food and water. His hands slid uselessly away from him, leaving him face down on the cold floor.

Pain ripped through his thigh as a piece of the broken jar cut deep into his leg. The warmth of his blood spread around the wound. Before he could push himself back up, another buzzing shock of energy hit him in the back, knocking all the air from his lungs.

Jacob gulped at the air, but his lungs seemed paralyzed. Domina's boots crunched the broken glass. The toe of her boot slid under his ribs and she kicked him onto his back.

"Don't you like playing with me?" Domina raised her foot in the dim torchlight. One of her stiletto heels glowed red like a hot iron. She pressed the glowing heel of her boot into Jacob's sternum. His lungs jolted back to life, only taking in enough air for him to scream.

Domina pulled her boot away and paced the room.

Jacob coughed on the acrid stench of his own burning flesh.

She smiled at him with a twinkle in her eye and said, "*Alescere.*"

For a moment, Jacob felt nothing. Then the floor beneath him began digging sharply into his flesh. The ground transformed into a bed of razor sharp nails, a thousand talons piercing his skin.

He rolled onto the smooth floor to his right, the nails biting his flesh and tearing the entire right side of his body open. Blood oozed down Jacob's back as he lay panting on the floor, watching the spikes continue to grow. He forced himself onto his knees when Domina started laughing again.

Domina reached down and grabbed Jacob's chin. "Don't be angry with me, love. I've done nowhere near my worst yet." She knelt in front of Jacob and gazed at him lovingly. "All I have to do to break you is tell you Emilia is being taken to her tethering ceremony right now."

Jacob shook his head, trying to make sense of Domina's words.

"She's all dressed up in her pretty white dress. And soon she'll be marched down the aisle." Domina started singing the wedding march. "*Flagrosa.*" She pulled flower petals from the air and tossed them onto Jacob. He barely registered the pain as they sizzled on his skin like boiling water.

"You're lying," Jacob growled, fighting to push himself off the ground. "Emilia would never agree to tether herself to anyone."

"Shh." Domina placed a finger over his lips. "I never said she agreed to anything. In a few minutes, she'll be joined eternally to Dexter Wayland. She will never be yours, my love. You will never save your sweet Emilia."

Rage flooded through Jacob. He screamed and grabbed Domina's neck. She laughed and batted his hands away, but angry red burns marked where his fingers had been.

"I suppose you have some magic in you after all." Domina

stood, running her fingers over the marks on her neck. "You may be my new favorite plaything."

"*Fulguratus!*" Jacob screamed, sending a bolt straight toward Domina's heart.

Domina gasped, her smile growing as Jacob's bolt hit her in the chest. "You'll have to try harder. But I can teach you. We'll have plenty of time. *Fulguratus.*"

Jacob fell back when her bolt hit him in the neck. He choked, struggling to pull in air. He tried to push himself up, but his arms shook, unable to hold his weight.

Domina's laugh filled the room as she tipped Jacob's head back and knelt on his chest. "We all have our destinies, Jacob. Yours is with me. And Emilia's is with him."

"No!" Jacob shouted. Fear and anger burned within him as magic began racing through his veins.

Domina's smile flickered for a moment before the room filled with a light so bright it blinded Jacob. Fire seemed to burst through his skin, and Domina's weight lifted from his chest. A horrible *crack* shook the room. Then everything went black.

Jacob lay gasping on the floor. "*Inluesco.*"

In the shadows cast by the dim light of his spell lay Domina, sprawled on the stone, blood pooling around her head.

Jacob pushed himself up, not taking his eyes off of her, waiting for her to spring back up laughing and trying to hurt him again. But she didn't move.

He crawled over, ignoring the pain and the blood dripping from his own wounds.

She lay still. Her eyes wide open and empty.

Jacob swallowed hard and tried not to move her as he pulled his wand from her belt. He pointed the wand at her chest and pulled the triangle of glass from his thigh, ready to use it as another weapon. Still she did not move. Blood pounded in his ears.

Domina was dead. He had killed her.

Jacob shook. He pulled off his shirt and wrapped it around his thigh to staunch the blood flowing freely from his wound. He almost stood before deciding to take Domina's ring as well. Bile rose in his throat when he touched her still-warm hand.

Jacob stumbled to the wall where Domina had entered not even ten minutes before. He ran his hands along the rough stone wall, searching for a knob or button, anything to let him out of this room. The tip of his wand grazed the wall in his search, and instantly the door appeared and began to open. Jacob steadied himself, hoping there were no guards and praying he could find Emilia in time.

30

THE TETHERING

*T*he hallway had been carved of roughly hewn rock. Unlike Jacob's cell, caged light bulbs lit the passage.

Jacob peered carefully out of his cell door. There were no guards in sight. He didn't know if Domina had sent them away for privacy, or if he simply wasn't considered a threat.

He looked up and down the hallway. The passage curved, its path only visible for about thirty feet in either direction. Even if he had been conscious when he was brought in, it wouldn't necessarily be the same path that would lead him to Emilia.

He swore under his breath and headed right. His leg wasn't working very well. His ankle wouldn't flex, and each time he put weight on his leg, more blood pulsed out through his wounds. He was leaving a trail of blood, but he hadn't learned any healing spells yet. That seemed like a really stupid thing not to have covered in his lessons.

After about fifty yards, Jacob came to another corridor crossing the one he was traveling. They both looked the same, but the branch to his left had more wires running along the ceiling than the others. If the Pendragon were going to have a tethering ceremony for Emilia, it would be in the grandest room these tunnels had to offer.

Jacob followed the wires. He turned left, right, right again, then left. But still, he met no one in the halls. The lack of obstacles pinged his nerves. Was he heading farther into the compound? Did they know where he was and just not care? Jacob pushed himself to move faster, pain and panic making him dizzy. How large was this place?

He was about to go back and try a different path when he turned the next corner and voices echoed down the hall. Lots of them. He slowed and moved closer to the wall, preparing for an ambush. But the voices were laughing and chatting.

Jacob glanced around the corner, expecting to see another corridor, but instead discovered a large chamber. This room had been left in its natural state. Stalactites hung from the ceiling, and stalagmites grew from the floor, creating large spikes and columns all around the room. Jacob scanned the chamber. It was the size of a small cathedral and just as grand. Over the centuries, the cave had made itself as beautiful as any man-made creation.

At least fifty people had congregated in the room. Jacob had definitely found the right place.

Dexter stood next to a chair in the center of the chamber.

Jacob lowered himself painfully to his knees and crawled behind a mound that had formed at the base of a grouping of stalagmites. He inched around, finding an angle where his body was hidden from the door, but he was still able to peer over the slippery stone at Dexter.

A horrible scream echoed from an entrance in the far wall of the chamber. Jacob recognized the scream at once.

Emilia, but she didn't sound hurt. She sounded furious.

Dexter turned and stared at the entrance, all of the blood draining from his face. Two men entered carrying Emilia, who was dressed in a long, gauzy white gown.

Her wedding gown.

Emilia's mouth was gagged, and her wrists were bound. One of the men carrying her bled badly from a bite on his ear. The other had claw marks on his face. She had done some damage before they tied her up.

Jacob's heart leaped into his throat at the sight of Emilia, alive and well enough to put up a fight.

A man followed Emilia and her captors into the hall, tall and wearing a jacket with a golden dragon emblazoned across the front. Everyone in the hall bowed as he entered.

So this is the Pendragon.

The Pendragon held up his hand, silencing the hall with a look. The two men carried Emilia over to a chair and forced her to sit. The one with the bloody ear said, "*Saxoris alescere.*" The stone floor surrounding Emilia's chair shifted. It was like watching a sped-up film of a flower's growth, only it was the stone that was growing, forming tall, thin tendrils that wrapped around Emilia, binding her to the chair. She screamed louder, struggling against the stone ropes, but they wouldn't budge.

"Friends," the Pendragon said, raising his voice only enough to be heard over Emilia's screams. He turned to Emilia. "*Oblitus.*"

Emilia still struggled, but her voice had vanished.

The Pendragon smiled and continued in a conversational tone. "Friends, we are here to witness the joining of my daughter, Emilia LeFay, to Dexter Wayland." He paused, and the crowd cheered.

Dexter stared at the still-struggling Emilia, his eyes wide and unblinking.

"Dexter," the Pendragon said, walking over to him, "I am entrusting you with my only child. It is for her safety and protection that I tether her to you. Are you willing to die to protect her?"

"Yes." Dexter looked Emilia in the eyes. "I would gladly die to protect her, Pendragon."

"Very well, my son," the Pendragon said. He touched Emilia's wrists, and the heavy iron cuffs fell into his hands and disappeared. Then he reached into his jacket and pulled out a golden cord, which he gave to Dexter. "Give one end to your *coniunx*."

Dexter took the cord and knelt in front of Emilia. "Please, Em. I know this seems like too much right now. But you have to know I would never do anything to hurt you. I love you." He pressed one end of the cord into Emilia's hand.

She threw it on the floor and continued to strain against her bonds.

Dexter winced as though Emilia had struck him. Sweat beaded on his forehead, glistening in the light.

"I am not cruel," the Pendragon said. "I know joining so young will be terrifying. Sixteen is such a tender age. But it cannot be helped, Emilia." He brushed her cheek. "My daughter, I do this for your protection. My friends, please proceed to the reception in the gallery. For two such tender children, a solemn tethering would be best."

Jacob lowered himself to the ground. The crowd's footsteps traveled away from him through the entrance in the far wall. When the footsteps were gone, Jacob pushed himself back up. The only people left in the room were Emilia, Dexter, and the Pendragon.

The Pendragon waved his wand, and the end of the cord snapped back into Emilia's hand. The stone ropes binding her to the chair slithered around her fingers, trapping the cord in her hand. Dexter still gripped his end.

"Care for my daughter, and I will gladly accept you as my son," the Pendragon said. Then, with his head tipped back and his arms outstretched, he began the incantation. Light shone from the golden cord, and the Pendragon seemed to glow as well, oblivious to Emilia's silent cries.

Jacob slid out from behind the rock and limped as quietly as he could toward Emilia.

Dexter stared into Emilia's eyes.

Tears streamed down her face, the angry lines in her forehead screaming all the words she could not say.

"I love you," Dexter said, his voice thick with his own tears. "Emilia, this is the only way."

Jacob stumbled, and Dexter's head snapped toward him.

The Pendragon seemed entranced by the spell and unaware of what was happening around him, but Dexter was going to warn him. Without any thought of magic, Jacob wrenched the cord from Dexter's grasp and punched him hard in the face. Dexter fell, but Jacob suddenly felt as though he couldn't move.

Warmth flowed up his arm and into his chest. Heat surrounded Jacob's heart and spread through his veins. But it wasn't unpleasant. More like his blood had never flowed properly before. Like his body had never had enough oxygen to process.

He took a deep breath, his lungs expanding and pushing the magic through his blood more quickly. The golden glow from the cord radiated up from his hand and surrounded his body. Then the light pulled away from him, snapping back so only his hand glowed.

The Pendragon stopped chanting. Smiling, he lowered his arms and head. He opened his eyes and saw Jacob.

Before he had time to think about what he was doing, Jacob shouted, "*Alevitum!*" The Pendragon grunted as an invisible force hit him, throwing him into the unyielding cavern wall.

Jacob rushed to Emilia. "*Everto.*" The stone ropes that bound her shattered.

She reached up and pulled the gag from her mouth. "Jacob," she said, her eyes dazed as he pulled her to her feet. But Dexter had begun to stir.

"Here." Jacob pressed Domina's ring into Emilia's hand. "We have to go." He pulled Emilia out the door he'd snuck in through minutes before.

They ran down the hall, Emilia slipping the ring onto her

finger. Even in her long dress, she could run faster than Jacob. The longer he stayed on his injured leg, the worse the damage from the glass and nails seemed to get. Blood drenched his leg, and his right foot had gone cold.

Emilia tugged Jacob into a small and dimly lit corridor. "You need to be healed." She turned Jacob's back to her.

"Emi." He tried to turn around to look at her. Something was different. Something felt strange, and he knew deep down in his soul that seeing her face would fix everything. But she pushed him back against the wall.

"*Pelluere.* Who did this to you?" Emilia asked as she tried to mend his shredded calf. "How did you get here?"

"Domina. But I really don't think it's as bad as it looks," Jacob lied. It was definitely as bad as it looked, maybe worse. He could feel his calf mending itself, but since some of his muscle was missing, the process of pulling the remaining parts together was excruciating. His thigh suddenly felt as though Domina's red-hot wand were piercing his wound. "They captured me while I was trying to rescue you," he said through gritted teeth.

"Iz sent you alone?" Emilia asked as she spun him around and started working on the burn on his chest.

"Samuel came, too," he answered, his voice tight from the pain of his healing wounds. He gasped as the burn on his chest stung like someone had pressed dry ice to it.

"Do they have him, too?" Emilia asked.

Jacob swore as his cheek started healing. "I don't know. He disappeared before I was captured, and that was at least two days ago. Domina never mentioned finding someone else."

Jacob's stomach sank. If they were very lucky, no one had realized they had escaped yet. But soon everyone would be looking for them. If they stopped to figure out if Samuel had been captured, they wouldn't have enough time to escape. The best they could do was hope Samuel was waiting for them outside.

"Do you know how to get out of here?" Emilia looked around as though searching for an exit sign.

"No, I was knocked out when they brought me in," Jacob said, trying to push past the other thoughts racing through his mind. "I followed the wiring to find you. The biggest wires went to that chamber you were in. The power has to come from somewhere. Maybe if we follow the wires, they'll lead us to the generator."

"And the generator should be near the exit so it can be easily fueled," Emilia finished for him. She frowned at Jacob's wounds. "This is the best I can do for now. Samuel can heal the rest."

They moved back out into the main corridor and continued to follow the wires. They had still seen no one. Emilia took the lead, peering around every curve.

A voice boomed through the halls, and Jacob pinned Emilia to the wall, covering her with his own body. The magnified voice of the Pendragon echoed, banging into their eardrums.

"The prisoner and traitor Jacob Evans has kidnapped my child. Guards, proceed to the compound entrance. All others search the caverns. Emilia is to be rescued unharmed. Anyone who damages her in any way shall answer directly to me. Jacob Evans may be killed on sight. The person who succeeds in destroying him will be generously rewarded."

Emilia looked at Jacob with terror in her eyes. She grasped his hand and pulled him down the corridor. Jacob limped behind as quickly as his leg would allow.

Their only hope was to make it to the entrance before the guards. The tunnel climbed steeply upward. Jacob was sure they had to be nearing the surface. They rounded a corner and almost ran right into the generator, but there was no opening to the outside world. They had hit a dead end.

Voices called in the distance. There was no chance of going back the way they had come.

"I'm sorry," he whispered.

They were trapped. There was no way out.

He hadn't saved her.

31

KILL ON SIGHT

*E*milia met Jacob's eyes.

Kill on sight. They had been ordered to kill him on sight.

"No," Emilia said, "we're getting out." She was not going to let Jacob die boxed in like an animal. Emilia surveyed the room. Maybe if they could find someplace to hide, they could wait for the searchers to go far enough back down the corridor that she and Jacob could find another way out.

Emilia scanned the room for a big enough hiding place. She froze when she spotted a pipe running up through the ceiling. The pipe had *diesel only* painted on it.

"Jacob, I need you to trust me." She moved in front of him and wrapped his arms around her waist like they were posing for prom pictures. "Do not move. *Primurgo.*" The air around them shimmered, and the shouts down the hall became strangely muffled.

Emilia placed her hand on the shield she had created and gently pressed through, careful not to tear the barrier. "Don't move." She aimed at the ceiling. "*Magneverto!*" She said the word and yanked her hand back through the shield just as the gas pipe exploded.

The blast tore through the room. The floor shook as orange flames encased their safe haven. Warmth flared over her skin, but even though the raging flames were mere inches from them, they did not get burned.

A dull *crack* pounded overhead as the ceiling around the pipe splintered like broken ice.

Jacob hunched over her, trying to protect her from the falling rocks. For a moment, the whole world shook. And then there was only dust.

"*Inluesco.*"

A light shone inside the spell's dome. Dust fell gently around them like a snow globe. Only the shaking snow was on the outside, and they were on the inside watching.

She lowered the shield and coughed, covering her mouth and nose with her hand to block some of the dust.

Rubble surrounded them. People screamed in the distance. The cave-in had affected more than just the generator room.

How many people did I hurt? Emilia wondered as another scream reached her ears.

"I think we can climb out." Jacob pointed to a dim light overhead. He started clambering up the rocks.

Emilia climbed after him. She slipped on her dress, and Jacob reached down and caught her hand without looking. The instant their hands met, Emilia's heart began to race, and at the same moment, her fear disappeared. Emilia pulled her hand away quickly and kept climbing.

"It's the sun," Jacob said. "I can see the sunset." Carefully, he shifted a few rocks and made the hole large enough for them to climb through. He pulled himself out and reached back for Emilia.

As her head broke through the dust and rocks, she took deep, gulping breaths of the fresh, clean air. The light from the setting sun burst through the trees. They were on a pile of rocks above a clearing. Chanting carried from below them, but through the trees, there was a way out.

"Come on," Emilia whispered and began to run for the forest.

"No!" Jacob shouted.

Emilia spun around, certain someone was attacking Jacob. He ran over to her and knocked her to the ground, hiding behind the rocks.

But the damage had been done. The guards had heard Jacob's shout.

"We have to run!" Emilia said, desperately trying to pull Jacob to his feet.

Jacob yanked Emilia back to the ground. "There's a shield. It'll fry you. There are chanters keeping it up." Jacob pointed past the rise. The sound of sliding rocks reached them as the guards struggled up the hill.

Emilia scrambled toward the top of the rocks, and Jacob followed. She looked at the circle. All she needed was one good spell to distract them.

But the guards were up the hill and closing in behind them. She screamed as one of them aimed a spell at Jacob that missed by mere inches. She pushed Jacob behind her using her own body as a shield.

"Stop!" one of the guards yelled. "Hand over the girl."

"I will not be handed to anyone," Emilia growled.

"The Pendragon is waiting for you inside. Come with us now."

They were surrounded with guards in front and a ledge behind. Jacob's arm slid around her waist. "Jump back on three," he whispered in her ear.

"One."

"Your father will be most displeased if you resist rescue," the guard said.

"Two."

"You are assisting the enemy and dishonoring the Pendragon."

"Three!"

They jumped backward and were in the air for only a moment before they hit the ground hard and fell over. The guards shouted from the rocks above. Only the two guards at the door had been left below.

"*Fulguratus!*" Jacob cried, and one of the guards fell.

"*Sporactus!*" Emilia shouted. The second guard's eyes went blank, and he swayed for a moment before crumpling to the ground.

Spells showered on them from above. Emilia pushed Jacob into the shelter of the cave entrance and ran toward the chanters, hoping the guards wouldn't risk hurting her. She reached the circle and stomped on the nearest pair of clasped hands, effectively breaking the circle and the chanters' attention. For good measure, she kicked the chanter nearest her in the stomach and punched her in the back of the head.

"Jacob, run!" Emilia screamed and sprinted toward the woods.

Jacob's footfalls pounded the ground behind her. "Emi, the shield!" Jacob shouted.

Spells flew at them from behind, and Emilia didn't dare slow down. She had broken the circle. The shield should be gone. It had to be gone. She heard Jacob gasp when they hit the edge of the clearing, but nothing happened as they shot into the trees.

They were foxes being chased by vicious hounds. No matter how fast they ran, they would still be pursued. She didn't know where she was leading Jacob. She just ran.

Their pursuers gained ground. She had tried her best to heal Jacob, but he still couldn't outrun the guards. And she would not leave him to die in the woods.

A *crack* shook the air as a tree was hit by a badly aimed spell. Emilia stopped short, barely avoiding being crushed by a falling limb. That moment was all the guards needed.

"*Inflaresco!*"

The spell hit Jacob square in the back, and he flew forward, screaming in pain. As he hit the ground, his wand rolled away. "Emilia, run," he coughed. "Go!"

But Emilia stood her ground. She would never let them hurt Jacob, not while she had breath to fight.

The guard who had attacked Jacob fell first, his face bursting with boils that swelled over his eyes and blinded him instantly. Another guard pushed him aside and ran toward Emilia.

"*Crusura!*" Emilia shouted.

The guard's legs snapped together, and he toppled headfirst over a fallen tree.

Just as Emilia was about to turn back to Jacob, a rough hand clasped her wrist and yanked her around. The guard opened his mouth to perform a spell.

Emilia aimed Domina's ring at the man's open mouth and cried, "*Sustaura!*"

The man dropped Emilia's hand as he tore at his own throat, gasping for air that wouldn't come.

The remaining guards circled Emilia, prowling like dogs. It didn't matter what she did; she was outnumbered. An arm wrapped around her throat. Emilia tried to kick, but someone else grabbed her feet. There was an agonizing snap in her finger as someone clawed at the ring Jacob had given her.

The guards threw her to the ground.

Fierce anger burned in Emilia's chest, cutting through her fear. A power and a magic that was not her own. "Jacob, no!" she tried to scream, but a knee on her throat blocked her air.

Then there was light. Bright, burning light. The weight from her body vanished. Emilia covered her face, trying to block out the blinding light. Heat pressed against her. The people around her dropped to the ground, screaming in fear and pain, but she remained unharmed. She heard the crackling of trees igniting. Smoke filled her nostrils.

The screaming stopped. She knew she should uncover her eyes, try to find Jacob, but she was too afraid.

He had lost his wand. She had seen it happen. Using that much magic without a talisman was suicide.

Tears welled in her eyes, breaking through eyelids she still held tightly shut. Emilia shook. A sob ripped through her throat. She could taste the ash in the air.

Jacob, her Jacob. Dead. He had made the ultimate sacrifice to protect her.

She sobbed uncontrollably. She didn't care who heard or who might be trying to attack. Opening her eyes meant seeing Jacob dead, and that would be far worse than anything the Dragons could do to her.

A hand brushed hers. "Emilia." Arms wrapped around her. Even through the smoke, she smelled fresh grass and peat.

She opened her eyes, and there was Jacob, alive and unharmed. The only thing that seemed wrong with him was the worried look on his face.

Emilia threw herself into his arms, crying even harder now. Jacob squeezed her tightly. "Emi, we have to go. I don't know if others might show up." He lifted her to her feet.

The tops of the trees were burning, their trunks stained black with soot. Jacob was right, they had to move, but Emilia couldn't let the whole forest burn. She'd been raised to believe in not harming innocents, even if the innocents were only animals. She closed her eyes and tried to calm herself.

"*Stinagro*," she said. The flames wavered for a moment and then flared up, stronger than before.

"*Stinagro!*" she said again. The flames didn't even flicker.

"We have to move." Jacob pulled on Emilia's elbow. But she was frozen, transfixed by the flames in front of her. "Emi, I'm sorry about the trees, but—" Jacob stopped short and stared white-faced at the solid wall of fire that had leaped up in front of them.

A fiery projection of the Pendragon gazed out of the flames.

32

THE FACE IN THE FLAMES

he flames spoke, spitting embers into the night, and the Pendragon's voice echoed through the burning forest.

"My child. I am sorry for what this vicious brute has done to you. You were destined to be joined with Dexter, and this blasphemer has stolen you for himself. Return to me, and I assure you I will reverse the tethering spell. Please do not let yourself be forever bound to this murderer. And he is a murderer. Look around you, Emilia. Look at what he has done."

Emilia stared into the flames, but Jacob couldn't tear his eyes from the bodies lying at his feet. All burned. All dead.

"Emilia, let me help you. Come home."

"Never!" Emilia screamed at the dancing flames.

"I am the only one who can reverse the spell," the flames hissed. "Right now, you find yourself drawn to this fiend, but it is only because of the tethering. Let me free you."

"The only way to undo a tethering is for one of the pair to die. Do you really think I don't know that?" Emilia spat.

"It must be done," the Pendragon replied without a hint of remorse.

"I will never let you hurt Jacob." Emilia stepped in front of Jacob, shielding him from the wall of fire.

"Then I am afraid I must do the only thing that I can. If you will not be saved, I must release you from your suffering." The flames leaped into the sky and started creeping toward Emilia. "Goodbye, my beloved." The face disappeared, but the flames continued to grow.

Emilia's warm hand closed around Jacob's and she dragged him down the mountain. The fire leaped from tree to tree, hissing and cracking with each new blaze. For a moment, Jacob thought they might outrun the flames, until the fire started licking the trees to his left and right.

They were being herded, penned in by the growing inferno. With every second, the open space in front of them grew smaller.

They ran, sliding and tripping down the mountain. Jacob's breath came in painful gasps as the smoke swam into his lungs.

He nearly fell when his feet hit hard, flat ground. They had found a road. Emilia kept leading him down the smooth pavement, and he ran as fast as he could, still moving awkwardly as pain shot through his wounded leg.

Emilia's grip slackened on his arm. She was bent almost double, choking on the smoke-filled air. Neither of them would make it much farther. Despite the brightness of the fire, the world dimmed in the haze of black smoke.

There was a roar in the distance, and light charged toward them. The fire was coming at them head on. The end had arrived. Jacob pulled Emilia behind him, determined that shielding her would be his final act. He stood ready to face the flames. But the lights were low, too low, and they weren't coming from the burning trees.

Tires squealed, and a black car stopped inches from Jacob. He braced himself, his lungs searing from the smoke. He swayed on his feet, exhaustion threatening to force him to the ground before a more magical enemy had the chance. Emilia moved to stand next to him, widening her stance, preparing to fight to the end.

Jacob choked in as much air as his lungs could bear and tried to steady himself. The only thing that kept him on his feet was Emilia at his side. She would fight to her last breath to protect him, and he would die if it meant even the slightest chance of her making it out of these woods alive.

The driver's door burst open, and Samuel jumped out. "Are you all right?"

"Samuel!" Emilia cried, running into his arms.

Samuel turned to Jacob. "Is there anyone else with you?"

"What?" Jacob shook his head.

Samuel stared into the blazing wall of flames marching steadily toward them. "Go," he said, pulling Emilia's arms from around him.

"Samuel." Emilia reached for Samuel's arm, but he was already running directly into the fire. "Samuel!" He didn't stop.

"Drive!" he yelled over his shoulder. "Drive, Jacob, and don't stop, no matter what!"

Emilia started to run after Samuel, but Jacob caught her around the waist and hauled her back to the car.

"No!" she screeched, kicking Jacob hard in the shins with her heel. "No! We have to get him back!"

But Samuel had already disappeared into the flames.

Jacob threw Emilia into the passenger seat and sealed the door with magic. He sprinted to the driver's side and climbed in. He fumbled with the gears for a moment, then took off down the mountain, thanking the fates the car was an automatic.

The smoke was so thick he could barely see the road. The farther down the mountain he drove, the closer the flames crept. No witches or wizards came through the trees, but horrible howls and screams pierced the night.

"The animals," Emilia whispered. "They're trapped."

Jacob slammed on the brakes when a deer ran in front of

them. Fire had found the creature. Flames streamed behind it like a cape of fiery death. The poor creature didn't even notice the car in its fear and pain. It just ran. Not realizing more flames waited for it through the trees.

His hands trembled as he pressed on the gas. Emilia turned and retched into the seat behind her.

He did as Samuel had ordered and sped down the mountain. Up ahead, the flames tried to reach across the road to close the circle. They leaped from treetop to treetop like small children trying to grab hands, but the gap between them was too wide. Jacob pushed the car as fast as it would go. Dangerously fast. And right as a flaming maple began to fall across the road, they passed out of the circle of fire.

A moment later, they were on the main road, but still Jacob didn't stop. He raced through the night, hoping against hope to find a highway that would lead home.

Why had Samuel left them? They could have fought together. He would have known the way home. Why would he run into the flames? Emilia sobbed, trembling in the seat next to him. There was no way they would ever know why Samuel went back, because there was no way he could make it out alive. They would never have a chance to ask him.

Jacob's body screamed from Domina's abuse. He wanted nothing more than to lie down and rest. But Emilia wouldn't be safe until they were back at the Mansion House, so he kept driving.

They found a highway Emilia recognized. The Dragons would know where they were going, but where else would they be safe?

When the sun began to kiss the sky, they turned onto the Mansion House drive. The car shuddered as they drove through the *fortaceria*, but they were allowed to pass. The house recognized Emilia. Now Iz would know they were coming.

As they pulled up to the house, the door burst open. Aunt Iz, the professor, Claire, Molly, Connor—everyone was there.

Almost.

Iz wrenched the car door open and wrapped Emilia in her arms. Molly came to Jacob's door and yanked him out, and Claire flung herself at him, oblivious to the sweat, blood, and ash covering him.

Molly peered into the car, but there was no one else to greet. She stifled a cry. "Samuel?"

"I am so sorry, Molly." Emilia reached for Molly, but Iz grabbed her hand. A streak on Emilia's palm still glowed gold.

Iz stared. Understanding dawned on every face except Claire's.

"What?" Claire pulled Emilia's hand from Iz. "What is that?"

"Oh, Emilia," the professor said. "How? Who did this?"

"LeFay. He's the Pendragon. Oh, Iz." Emilia sobbed, her whole body shaking.

Jacob stumbled to Emilia and wrapped his arms around her, wanting to hold her close enough to make everything all right. Emilia swayed, and Jacob scooped her into his arms and limped toward the house. Iz touched his arm to stop him, gasping when she saw his hand was also marked in gold. Tears glistened in her eyes as she nodded, letting him carry Emilia away.

~

The bedspread shifted under Emilia's back as he lowered her onto the bed. It smelled like flowers, soft and familiar. The swirling pattern on the quilt was the same as when she had left it.

But Emilia saw her blood-stained, gold-streaked hand and pushed herself off the bed, stumbled into the bathroom, and slammed the door behind her. She tried to scrub her hands. The sink flooded with red. Jacob's blood mixed with her own as it flowed down the drain. But who else's blood was on her hands? How many people had died because of her?

Sobs echoed in the bathroom, but they seemed too far away to be hers. All she wanted was to wash the evidence of the past five days from her hands. Her wrists were raw and bloody from struggling against her bindings, but the palm of her left hand would never heal. The gold mark was permanent.

She staggered to the shower and turned the water on as high and hot as it would go. She didn't even take off her clothes. Someone pounded on the door, but she didn't answer. She stood under the water, letting it burn her. The tears running down her cheek mixed with the burning water, leaving no trace they had ever existed. They were simply swept away.

Another tear came, and then another. An unending line of salty soldiers that swirled to their deaths in the drain. She wanted nothing more than to slip down the drain and follow her tears into oblivion. She sobbed so hard it felt as though her ribs would crack and her lungs explode. She knelt in the shower and grieved for Samuel. For Dexter, who was lost to her forever. For the mother she'd never known, and for her father, whom she would fight to her last breath to destroy.

Emilia hadn't heard the door *bang* open, hadn't noticed a hand reach in to cool the scalding water. But Jacob's arms were around her. He smoothed her hair and held her to his chest. He didn't try to stop her tears. He just held her and let her mourn for the happy life to which she could never return.

33

WHAT WAS LOST

*J*acob had wrapped her in a robe. It was fuzzy and warm and blue. Emilia knew it was her robe, but it felt foreign to her, like she'd borrowed the memory of owning it from someone else's life. There were too many fresh and horrid memories for the old ones to hold much meaning now.

Jacob handed her a comb. She stared at his hand. The hand that had lost his wand. But the spell—he had done the spell anyway. And he was still here and alive.

"How?" Emilia asked, meeting Jacob's eyes. "How did you do it?"

"Emilia—"

"How did you do that spell?"

Jacob didn't answer her. Emilia wanted to scream, to run, to know why. Why had this happened to her? To them?

"Jacob," she whispered, "tell me." Tears crept into the corners of her eyes again. She needed an answer to something. And there was no one else to ask any of her other questions. Emilia pulled away from him.

"I don't know," Jacob said as he grabbed her shoulder. "Emilia, I really don't. Please."

Emilia refused to turn around.

"The Dragons had you, and I knew there was no way out. I heard you scream, and I had to protect you. So I did the spell without the wand. I knew I would die without a talisman, and I didn't even really formulate a spell, I just wanted to protect you. And I felt the energy surge, and I thought I was dead. But then everyone was gone but you and me." He paused and walked around to face her. He tilted her chin up and brushed her damp hair away. "I don't know how I did it. But I don't care. You're safe."

Emilia didn't want to meet his eyes. The gold streak glowed on his palm. There was an angry red scar over his heart. Another mark no spell could heal.

She had almost lost him.

Emilia touched the burn on his cheek. "We're safe." And she tucked her head onto his shoulder.

~

*J*acob lay in bed. Emilia had finally fallen asleep, her head curled on Jacob's chest. He brushed the hair off her cheek. He wanted to stay with her and sleep himself away from the pain.

But the danger wasn't over. Aunt Iz needed to know everything. The more information she had, the safer they would all be.

He slid Emilia's head onto her pillow and crept into the hall. Voices drifted from the kitchen, but he continued to Iz's study. She needed to know first.

Iz's door waited open. Dim light spilled into the hall. He didn't knock. He couldn't bear the thought of asking permission to enter the study to deliver this sort of news.

Iz sat behind her desk, staring at her wrinkled hands, apparently waiting for Jacob. An untouched sandwich and full cup of tea sat on the desk.

"How is she?" Iz asked without looking up.

"Asleep." Jacob sat in the chair across from the desk. The same chair he had sat in the day Iz asked him if he wanted to be a wizard. It hadn't even been two months. It felt like a lifetime. Lives had changed, and lives had ended.

Jacob didn't know where to begin, so he sat in silence, waiting for Iz to look at him.

Finally, she did. "Where is Samuel?"

Jacob explained about the shield and Samuel leaving to call for help. He told her about the tattoo and using the airplane man to sneak into the compound, and about Samuel finding them and running back into the circle.

"He is a very brave man," Iz said. "He may still be alive. Samuel is an excellent warrior. I will not give up hope."

Jacob didn't say anything. He couldn't imagine anyone surviving that fire and fighting the Dragons.

"Jacob?" Iz asked after a few moments. "How did the tethering happen?"

The chamber in the caves flashed in his thoughts. All the wizards watching Emilia being tied down. Dexter holding a golden cord. His hands started to shake, and one was streaked in gold. He clenched it into a tight fist to hide the mark, forcing himself to breathe. He didn't want his fear to wake Emilia. "The Pendragon tried to tether Emilia to Dexter."

"Dexter is with the Dragons?"

Jacob nodded.

Iz stood and paced.

"I tried to stop the ceremony," Jacob said, "and ended up becoming a part of the spell."

"Why would the Pendragon want to tether Emilia and Dexter? Did Dexter request the ceremony? Was Emilia a reward for him?"

"I don't think he wanted to do it. The Pendragon arranged it."

"Why?" Iz waited as Jacob struggled with the words.

"The Pendragon. He's Emilia's father."

Iz stopped mid-stride.

"He said he was doing what was best for Emilia. That he was trying to protect her."

Iz walked over, took Jacob's left hand in hers, and turned his palm to examine it. "How are you? Tethering is—"

"I'm fine." Jacob pulled his hand away.

"Tethering can change how you feel," Iz said quietly, "and it can never be undone."

"I don't feel any different. My world has been centered around Emilia for a long time. The only difference is now it feels physical." He rubbed his ribs just above his heart, ignoring the pain from Domina's burn. "I feel a pull in my chest toward her. And I know she's still asleep because I can feel how calm she is. But I still love her, just like always."

Jacob stood. He needed to rest, to drift away from all the questions. To be closer to Emilia.

But he turned back in the doorway. "The problem is, she was never in love with me. And now, even if she does want to be with me someday, I'll never know if she really loves me or if it's just part of some spell. They took her choice away from her, but I made mine a long time ago."

Jacob turned and walked down the hall.

The banister glowed in the afternoon sun as he climbed the stairs. He walked down the girls' wing and into Claire's room, picked up her fluffy pink chair, and set it outside Emilia's door. He lay back in the chair and closed his eyes.

They needed rest, but he would be there when she woke up.

Jacob and Emilia's journey continues in The Siren's Realm.

JACOB AND EMILIA'S JOURNEY
CONTINUES IN THE SIREN'S REALM

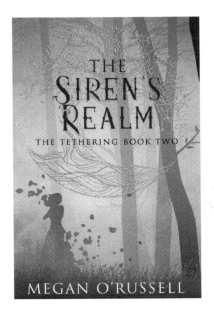

Read on for a sneak peek of *The Siren's Realm.*

BOUND

*T*he cool autumn air crept through the house. The trees in the garden had not yet begun to change their leaves, but they seemed to know their time was coming.

Inside the house was silence. As the afternoon sun peered through the window, all it saw was stillness. Emilia sat at her desk in the big library, staring at a page in a little brown book.

TETHERING

The magical binding of two people. Historically, tethering was an integral part of a wizarding wedding. After a tethering ceremony, the coniunx, or tethered couple, would gain the ability to sense one another and would develop a greatly increased emotional attachment.

In today's wizarding society, tethering is rarely included in wedding ceremonies. It is generally considered archaic and makes divorce much more difficult, as a tethering can only be severed by the death of one of the coniunx. The demise of half of the pair is incredibly painful for the remaining party and often results in their subsequent death.

Throughout wizarding history, some have used tethering as a weapon. By forcing a slave, captive, or unwilling bride to be tethered to a new master, the spellcaster would ensure the forcibly tethered party would be unlikely to attempt escape, and should an escape occur, tracking the coniunx *would be simple. Forced tethering was made illegal in 1813 as a part of the International Wizarding Agreement and is punishable by the severest penalty allowable in the nation in which the offense occurs.*

Captive. Unable to escape. How many times had she read that page in the few months since Graylock? Five hundred, maybe six? Reading the passage never made it any better. Still, she began the page again, hoping the words would somehow be different.

Tethering—The magical binding of two—

The front door crashed open, and an excited shout of "Emilia!" carried down the hall followed closely by, "Claire, don't break the door!"

Emilia slipped the book into the desk drawer before Claire tore around the corner and into the library.

"Emilia!" she squealed, her bright blond hair falling from her ponytail, and her cheeks red from excitement and the wind. "You missed the best thing ever! I helped Jacob with his shield spells, and I sparred with Connor and won!"

Claire began an energetic victory dance as Jacob and Connor entered the library. Connor limped in with a grimace on his face, and Jacob failed to suppress a smile.

"Yes, Claire," Connor said through clenched teeth as he lowered himself into his desk chair, "you did a great job."

"What's that you say?" Claire leaned in toward Connor, her hand cupped around her ear. "You just got beat by a twelve-year-old?"

Emilia smiled, knowing it was what Claire wanted to see. Aunt Iz had always believed that all witches and wizards should know how to defend themselves. Sparring had been a part of the education received at the Mansion House for as long as Emilia could remember, but daily practice hadn't begun until after Graylock. That's how life felt now, split into two pieces—before Graylock, and after.

Emilia noticed Claire's mouth moving. She bounced around,

giving a blow by blow of how she had beaten Connor. Claire stood on the back of the couch before launching herself onto Connor.

Emilia forced herself to laugh as cheerfully as she could manage. "That's great, Claire." She hoped her voice didn't sound too unnaturally high.

"Let's go get some dinner," Jacob said, lifting Claire off Connor, taking her by the shoulders and steering her toward the hall.

"But I want to talk to Emilia." Claire twisted away from Jacob's grasp.

"Later," Jacob said firmly. He jerked his head for Connor to follow and led Claire out of the library.

Emilia laid her forehead on her desk. The wood felt cool on her face. She should follow them. It was time for dinner. Molly would be waiting, but other faces would be missing. Everywhere she went in the house, someone was missing.

Emilia's heart started to race. She took a deep breath, but in her mind all she could see was flames. And Samuel and Dexter. They should be here. But Samuel was gone, and Dexter was a traitor.

"Emi." Jacob touched her back, sending her heart racing again, but in such a different way. She sat up and looked into Jacob's bright blue eyes.

"They're waiting for you," Jacob said, pulling his hand back as Emilia shrugged away from his touch.

"Sure." Emilia stood and started for the kitchen, but as she passed the dining room, a chorus of voices shouted, "Happy birthday!"

Aunt Iz, Molly, Professor Eames, Connor, and Claire all stood around the table looking at her. Emilia stared at them.

"You didn't think we would forget your birthday?" Aunt Iz asked, walking over to Emilia and pulling her into a warm hug.

"No, of course not." Emilia blinked away her confusion. She

didn't think they had forgotten her birthday, but she hadn't remembered it herself.

"Come sit!" Claire dragged Emilia away from Iz and pushed her into her seat at the table.

"Our little girl is seventeen already." Molly bustled out of the room, dabbing her face on her apron, and returned moments later with large plates of food hovering in front of her. As though held by invisible butlers, the plates all laid themselves down on the table with perfect synchronization. She hadn't cooked a meal like this since before Graylock.

"Claire worked all morning on the decorations," Connor said, pointing over Emilia's head and rolling his eyes as he began to eat.

Emilia twisted in her seat. A pink sign that had *Happy Birthday Emilia!!!!!!!!* written in glitter hung over the door. Pink confetti swirled through the air like snow, and three foot wide pink balloons bounced along the ceiling. The only concession to the fact that pink was not, in fact, Emilia's favorite color was the sole lavender balloon tied to the back of her chair.

Emilia looked around the room. Iz smiled back at her from the end of the table. Her grey hair was tied back in an elegant twist as always, but she looked older than she should. Her face was weathered with lines that had not been there a few months ago. Next to her sat Molly, covered with a light dusting of flour, her greying red hair falling out of its bun.

Next to Molly was Connor, her nephew, with bright red hair to match hers. Molly piled heaps of food onto his plate, continuously tutting about him growing too quickly, and she was right. He was fourteen and tall for his age. He had grown another two inches this month.

On Emilia's other side sat Claire, shaking her head at Professor Eames. The professor was shorter than everyone but Claire. His shrunken frame betrayed his age, but his toady little face was split in a wide grin as he chuckled and Claire giggled.

And Jacob. His dark blond hair needed cutting again. His bright blue eyes twinkled as he listened to Claire trying to explain something to the professor through her laughter.

Emilia knew they were all trying. They were being cheerful for her sake, giving her a happy birthday. But Emilia couldn't look away from the empty places at the table.

Claire had carried Dexter's chair to the yard and set fire to it months ago, as soon as she found out what Dexter had done. But Samuel's seat was still waiting for him at the table, like he was running late to her party and would come bounding in from the garden any minute.

Emilia talked with the family while they ate. Lessons they had done lately. Stories from when Molly was young. Perfectly normal conversation.

Molly brought out a huge cake covered with tiny flowers. In the center of each blossom was a candle burning with a vivid blue flame. As Emilia blew out the candles, each of the flowers floated into the air, joining the confetti that soared endlessly around the room, weaving in and out of the glistening chandelier.

"It's beautiful, Molly," Emilia said.

"Open your presents!" Claire shoved a box into Emilia's hands.

The box was small and covered in pale blue velvet. As Emilia opened it, her breath caught in her throat. Inside was a delicate silver ring with a tree of life, the crest of the Gray Clan, carved into the front.

"To replace the one that was lost," Iz said quietly. "I had it made by the same jeweler."

"Thank you, Aunt Iz." Emilia pushed her face into a smile.

"Now you can use it as your talisman again," Claire said, taking the ring out of the box and shoving it onto Emilia's finger.

"Maybe." Emilia touched the sapphire pendant around her neck. "I think I might try out my necklace a while longer."

Claire wrinkled her forehead.

"I love the ring, Aunt Iz. Thank you." Emilia stood and went over to Aunt Iz. She hugged her tight, trying to put so many things she hadn't been able to say into her arms.

"Jacob has a present for you, too," Claire said, handing Emilia a bigger box as soon as she broke away from Iz.

"Thank you, Jacob," Emilia said as she tore the white, sparkling paper off the box.

Inside was a mobile made of the brightest green leaves. As she pulled it out of the box, the leaves began to spin slowly as though blown by a gentle breeze. A sprig of lilac, Emilia's favorite flower, sat still at the very center as everything else rotated around.

Emilia remembered a night when Jacob had first come to the Mansion House, when he had first learned he was a wizard.

"Making the leaves fly was the first piece of magic you showed me here," Jacob said, pink creeping into his cheeks. "I put a *viriduro* spell on it so the flowers will always stay fresh."

"Well done." The professor leaned in to inspect the mobile.

"Thank you," Emilia said, touching Jacob's arm. His eyes met hers, and she pulled her hand away, sliding the mobile back into the box.

After an hour of dinner, Emilia's face ached from smiling. She hadn't spent that much time with anyone in months. Her brain felt heavy and tired from so much talking.

Molly had given her a new dress and a box of peanut brittle, and the professor had given her a new book on early African Wizards. When Molly finally started clearing the table, Emilia slipped away, running up the stairs to her room before anyone could call her back.

Emilia opened her bedroom window, letting the cold air fill the room. Thousands of stars peered back at her. The trees rustled in the breeze.

She lay down, gazing up at the canopy of her bed, trying to ignore the pull in her chest that told her to go and find Jacob. If she were with him, her heart said, everything would be all right. If she were with him, she would be safe.

Emilia gazed at the silver ring on her finger. She twisted her hand, watching the etched tree of life glint in the light. Where was her other ring, the one Iz had given her when she was seven? Had it been tossed aside in some cave? Was someone else using it as a talisman now? Using her ring to hurt people?

Jacob had given her a different ring to defend herself. One that felt almost exactly like this one. The same smooth band, the same feel on her hand.

Leaping off the bed, Emilia yanked open her dresser drawer and dug into the back corner where she had hidden the other silver ring. That ring had been contaminated, something found in an evil place. She had tossed it into the drawer without looking at it, wanting desperately to get it out of her sight.

Emilia's fingers closed on the cold metal, and she pulled the ring from the stacks of clothes. A silver ring, identical to hers except for the carving. Where hers had a tree, this ring had a tiny bird. A fist closed around her heart.

"Emilia!"

Footsteps thundered up the stairs. Cries of "Emilia!" and "Jacob, what's wrong?" echoed through the house.

Emilia's door burst open, and Jacob raced through, followed closely by Claire and Connor.

Jacob knelt next to Emilia, taking her face in his hands. She hadn't even noticed she was crying until he brushed the tears off her cheek.

"What's wrong?" he whispered.

"What's happening?" Aunt Iz asked as she and Molly panted into the room. The professor wheezed as he shuffled up next to them.

"I never looked at it." Emilia shook her head. Blond hair and a smiling rosy face swam through her mind. She held the ring out to Iz. "I put it away so I wouldn't have to see it. And now it's been so long." Emilia's voice cracked.

Iz took the ring and gasped.

"What?" Claire snatched the ring from Iz. Her eyes widened as they fell on the little bird. "Larkin. This is Larkin's ring. Why do you have Larkin's ring? She's missing. Did she leave it for you here? Is it a message from her?" Claire began tearing through Emilia's drawers. "She might have left something else. Larkin would leave us a clue so we could find her."

"She didn't leave it," Jacob said, wrapping an arm around Claire and pulling her away from the dresser. "I found that ring at Graylock."

"She was there," Emilia whispered. "That's why Samuel asked if we were alone. That's why he went back. To find her."

Larkin had been like a big sister to her, her protector. The Gray student who had become one of the elite MAGI Agents who protected order in the magical world.

Emilia yanked her hands through her hair. "He was going to save her, and we left both of them behind. Jacob, we left them."

"Emi." Jacob reached for her.

"We left them!" Emilia screamed, backing away from all of them. They didn't understand. It was her fault. Larkin was supposed to be indestructible. But MAGI had been ransacked by the Dragons, and Larkin taken at Graylock. Emilia had left them there. Samuel and Larkin, trapped in the dark. Her heart pounded in her chest, and sweat slicked her palms.

"Emilia, breathe," Aunt Iz said softly, just as she had when Emilia was little and lost control of her magic. But it wasn't Emilia who was spinning out of control. It was all of them. It was the world.

The mirror over Emilia's dresser shattered. Connor grabbed Claire and knocked her to the floor. Iz covered her head, the professor yelped, and Molly screamed. Jacob didn't flinch as he stared at Emilia.

"*Reparactus*," Jacob murmured, and the pieces of glass flew through the air back into their frame. Within seconds, the cracks in the mirror disappeared as if it had never been broken.

Emilia looked into the mirror at an unfamiliar face. The long black hair was hers, but the grey eyes were wild and afraid.

"We will find a way to get Samuel and Larkin back," Aunt Iz said, walking to Emilia and wrapping her arms around her.

"They've been in there for months. If you couldn't find a way to get Samuel out, how are you going to get two people out? It's my fault," Emilia choked.

Molly and the professor herded Claire and Connor out of the room. Jacob slipped out behind them.

"None of this would have happened," Emilia struggled to speak but couldn't get the words out through her gasping tears.

The sheets folded back as Aunt Iz guided her to bed, tucking her in as she had done when Emilia was little. But warm blankets couldn't keep the monsters away. Not anymore.

CLAIRE'S GIFT

*E*milia couldn't sleep. She could feel Jacob upstairs, waiting to be sure she was all right. The voices that traveled through the hall were hushed, as though Emilia were a patient with a fatal illness.

Hours passed.

The stars traveled outside her window. Emilia forced herself to breathe, willing herself to remain calm. She didn't want Jacob to come running.

The floorboard outside Emilia's room squeaked.

There was a light tap on the door, and Claire called softly, "Emilia, can I come in?"

Emilia pulled her covers up over her head. She was warm, and it was quiet. Her desire to be left alone warred against how hurt Claire's feelings would be if she ignored her.

"Emilia, are you awake?" Claire's voice came again.

Emilia forced herself to sit up, turned on the light, and arranged her face into a smile. "Come on in."

Claire poked her blond head around the door. Her forehead was furrowed, and her mouth set in a scowl.

"What's up?" Emilia asked.

Claire sat down next to Emilia on the pale purple comforter, clutching her pink laptop to her chest.

"Are you okay?" Claire asked, examining Emilia's face.

"I'm fine." Emilia hoped it sounded true.

"I have a birthday present for you, but I need to make sure you won't freak out and break anything," Claire said in an unusually businesslike tone.

"I promise not to hurt your computer," Emilia said.

Claire nodded, apparently satisfied, and loosened her grip on the pink laptop. "Good, but nobody can know about this. If Iz found out, I'd be dead or sent away in a second."

Emilia's face fell. "Claire, what did you do?"

"I didn't really *do* anything. I'm just not actually supposed to have it." Claire's voice dripped with guilt.

"Did you steal something from Iz?" Emilia asked.

"Not from Iz."

"Claire!"

"Shhh!" Claire clapped a hand over Emilia's mouth. "And it wasn't stealing as much as salvaging. When you were…away, and MAGI was attacked, Aunt Iz asked me to crash the Spellnet database. With no one in the MAGI offices to make sure the system was secure, anyone could have hacked into the files, taken whatever information they wanted, and no one would have known."

"You crashed Spellnet?" Emilia asked, impressed despite herself at Claire's computer skills.

"Absolutely. Really, it was a piece of cake. MAGI wasn't as up on their security as they should have been, so crashing Spellnet wasn't that hard. I deleted their information and then ran a virus that fried the system," Claire said.

"Well, if that's what Iz wanted you to do, she can't be mad at you for doing it. I'm sure you'll be fine," Emilia said, rubbing Claire's back.

"That's not the part where I get sent home." Claire opened her vividly pink laptop and started the process of opening her encrypted files. "Before I deleted the files, I may have reallocated some of them to my computer."

"Reallocated?" Emilia raised her left eyebrow.

"You know you look a lot like Aunt Iz when you do that?"

Emilia's eyebrow climbed even higher.

"Fine, I stole some information. It seemed a pity to throw *all* of it out when we could use it to do some actual good in this cold, hard world."

"What exactly did you take, Claire?" Emilia tried to keep her tone level.

"A few things. The information on Wizard-owned patents, the Spellnet Satellite codes, and the registered Witch and Wizard database."

"Claire, that information is confidential."

"I'm not going to go flashing it around if that's what you're worried about. And besides, you should be grateful. I found something I think will interest you. Unless, of course, you don't want your present?" She paused. When Emilia didn't respond, Claire continued. "I didn't think so. I went through the files of registered Witches and Wizards. I found your father's file." Claire clicked on a folder labeled *Emile LeFay*. "And I think"—Claire took a deep breath—"I found your mother."

Emilia froze. "Claire, LeFay didn't tell me her name. Iz doesn't know who she was. She tried to find her. She asked MAGI for help."

"Iz didn't have free range over the files. And they weren't completely computerized then. All I had to do was enter disappearances around your birthday. It was a lot easier than I thought it would be. I had plans for all kinds of ways to search for her. She was one of only five reported missing around that time, and she was the only girl." Claire clicked open a file.

A photo labeled *Rosalie Wilde* stared out from the screen. The girl in the picture had long, black hair that hung in heavy curls. Her features were smaller than Emilia's, and her eyes were blue instead of grey, but Emilia knew in an instant that Claire was right. Rosalie Wilde was her mother.

"What does it say about her?" Emilia brushed the tears away from her eyes so they wouldn't blur her view of the screen.

"She was a runaway. She and LeFay were apprenticed in the same house. He graduated, and she ran away three weeks later. Her family asked MAGI to help find her. It looks like MAGI put out a few inquiries." Claire scrolled down to a scanned document with dates and contacts, a record of MAGI's failed attempts to locate Rosalie. "They didn't do much until after there were a few murders reported near the Graylock Preserve."

Dark mountains and flames flooded Emilia's mind.

"Over the course of five months, two of the wizards who were listed as missing at the same time as your mother were found dead, along with five humans. A couple matching LeFay's and Rosalie's descriptions were seen in the area. That's when MAGI really started looking for her."

"Because they thought she was a murderer," Emilia said dryly.

"There's no evidence I can find that ties her to any of the deaths, and both of the wizards' deaths were ruled accidental."

"LeFay is a murderer, and if Rosalie was there, she must have been helping him." Emilia pushed herself off the bed and started pacing. She never should have let Claire come in. Being alone was better than this.

"But she left, Em."

Emilia's neck tensed. "Please don't call me that."

That was what Dexter had called her. She hated the sound of it now.

"Okay, Emilia. I won't," Claire said quietly. She was silent for a minute while Emilia continued to pace the room. "These records say Rosalie left Graylock right after the first bodies were found. MAGI started looking for LeFay and Rosalie. LeFay never surfaced, but there were sightings of Rosalie.

"She was seen in a small town in Massachusetts two months after she disappeared from the preserve. Then nothing for about six months. After that, she was seen in California, New York City, and the last sighting was in Maine five months after you were born." Claire closed the laptop and watched Emilia's progress back and forth across the room.

"Thank you, Claire," Emilia said, not looking at her. "Thank you for finding this for me."

"Every time your mom was seen, there was no sign of LeFay. And they were looking for him, too. I think she really did leave him. Emilia, if her birthday on file is right, she was only eighteen when she had you. But she left LeFay. She ran away, alone and pregnant." Claire stood and hugged Emilia, stopping her from moving. "I think she got scared of him and ran. I think she was trying to protect you. If she thought what he was doing was right, she would have stayed with him. It would have been easier. I really think she loved you. I wanted you to know."

Emilia wrapped her arms around Claire. "Thanks, Claire. It's nice to know her name."

"No problem," Claire said, brushing the tears from Emilia's cheek, "and I made a whole file about her. It kind of made me feel like a creeper, but when you want it, let me know." Claire picked up her laptop and started for the door.

"What happened to her?" Emilia asked, not sure she wanted an answer.

"The MAGI trail ends in Maine. But I can work on finding out more if you want."

"That would be great." Emilia nodded. "But don't tell anyone."

"Our secret." Claire smiled and slipped into the dark hall, closing the door silently behind her.

Emilia flopped down onto the bed. Rosalie Wilde. Scared, eighteen, mother? Or evil, wizard supremacist, murderer? She pulled her pillow over her face. All she could see was the smiling, blue-eyed girl, only a year older than herself. But LeFay was eighteen once, too.

Order The Siren's Realm *to continue the story.*

ESCAPE INTO ADVENTURE

Never miss a moment of the danger or romance.

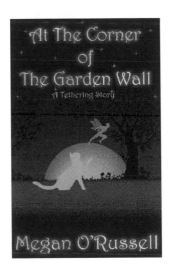

There were more than three students out of bed the night Jacob got his wand. Discover Claire's adventure in *At The Corner of the Garden Wall*, available exclusively to members of the Megan O'Russell Readers Community. Visit https://www.meganorussell.com/claire to sign up!

If you enjoyed *The Tethering*, please consider leaving a review to help other readers find Jacob and Emilia's story.

As always, thanks for reading,

Megan O'Russell

ABOUT THE AUTHOR

Megan O'Russell is the author of several Young Adult series that invite readers to escape into worlds of adventure. From *Girl of Glass*, which blends dystopian darkness with the heart-pounding danger of vampires, to *Ena of Ilbrea*, which draws readers into an epic world of magic and assassins.

With the *Girl of Glass* series, *The Tethering* series, *The Chronicles of Maggie Trent*, *The Tale of Bryant Adams*, the *Ena of Ilbrea* series, and several more projects planned for 2020, there are always exciting new books on the horizon. To be the first to hear about new releases, free short stories, and giveaways, sign up for Megan's newsletter by visiting the following:

https://www.meganorussell.com/book-signup.

Originally from Upstate New York, Megan is a professional musical theatre performer whose work has taken her across North America. Her chronic wanderlust has led her from Alaska to Thailand and many places in between. Wanting to travel has fostered Megan's love of books that allow her to visit countless new worlds from her favorite reading nook. Megan is also a lyricist and playwright. Information on her theatrical works can be found at RussellCompositions.com.

She would be thrilled to chat with you on Facebook or

Twitter @MeganORussell, elated if you'd visit her website MeganORussell.com, and over the moon if you'd like the pictures of her adventures on Instagram @ORussellMegan.

ALSO BY MEGAN O'RUSSELL

The Girl of Glass Series
Girl of Glass
Boy of Blood
Night of Never
Son of Sun

The Tale of Bryant Adams
How I Magically Messed Up My Life in Four Freakin' Days
Seven Things Not to Do When Everyone's Trying to Kill You
Three Simple Steps to Wizarding Domination

The Tethering Series
The Tethering
The Siren's Realm
The Dragon Unbound
The Blood Heir

The Chronicles of Maggie Trent
The Girl Without Magic
The Girl Locked With Gold
The Girl Cloaked in Shadow

Ena of Ilbrea
Wrath and Wing
Ember and Stone
Mountain and Ash

Ice and Sky

Feather and Flame

<u>Guilds of Ilbrea</u>

Inker and Crown

Made in the USA
Middletown, DE
19 December 2020

28721371R00149